Cruise Ship Cozy Mystery

Series Book 2

Hope Callaghan

http://hopecallaghan.com
Copyright © 2015
All rights reserved.

A special thank you to Wanda Downs and Peggy Hyndman for taking the time to read and review the second book in my new series, *Portside Peril*, and offering all of the helpful advice!

Visit my website for new releases and special offers: http://hopecallaghan.com

TABLE OF CONTENTS

Chapter 1

Chapter 2

Chapter 3

Chapter 4

Chapter 5

Chapter 6

Chapter 7

Chapter 8

Chapter 9

Chapter 10

Chapter 11

Chapter 12

Chapter 13

Chapter 14

Chapter 15

Chapter 16

Chapter 17

Chapter 18

Chapter 19

Chapter 20

Chapter 21

Chapter 22

Chapter 23

Chapter 24

Chapter 25

Banana Nut Bread

About The Author

Chapter 1

"Cat is madder than a wet hornet!"

Millie Sanders, Assistant Cruise Director, had just stuck her key card in the cabin door slot and reached for the handle when her friend, Annette Delacroix, came up behind her.

Millie turned around. "Really?" She *had* been having a good day. Actually, she'd been having a great day but things were suddenly taking a turn for the worse.

"Let me guess. She's mad at me?" Millie held out a little hope that maybe Cat wasn't angry with her for throwing her under the bus, so to speak.

Annette clucked her tongue. "You should see her! She's up in the gift shop, tearing the place apart, hair flying everywhere."

Millie pressed her hands to her cheeks. This was bad. It was worse than she had expected.

1

Catherine Wellington's signature beehive hairdo was always perfectly coiffed with nary a hair out of place.

"W-what's she saying?" Millie squeezed her eyes shut and offered up a quick prayer.

"Something about a traitorous, two-timing, double-dealing, skunk-smelling."

Millie cut her off. "I get the idea." Her shoulders sagged. There was no way Millie could live onboard the cruise ship with an archenemy – namely Cat - who had a tendency to gossip. If Cat set her mind to it, Millie was 100% certain she could make Millie's life miserable.

"I guess I better go try to make amends." Millie pulled her key from the slot and shoved it into her pocket. She followed Annette down the corridor.

Millie eyed her friend. "What about you? You're just as guilty as I am," she pointed out.

Annette nodded. "True, but for some reason, you're the target." Annette shrugged her shoulders. "Better you than me!"

Annette and Millie had set up a sting to catch a potential killer. Cat had walked right into their trap. In the end, police cleared Cat, but not before she spent some time behind bars, which was the reason for her fit of rage, directed at Millie.

Millie opened the door that separated the crew quarters from the guest area. She held the door and waited for Annette to step through.

Annette shoved her hands in her pockets. "I'd love to go with you. You know, help smooth things out but I've gotta get up to the kitchen. Something about a fish fiasco."

Millie stopped in the hall. She crossed her arms and pursed her lips as she glared at Annette.

"If it doesn't work out, let me know and I'll try to talk to her," Annette offered.

Millie watched her friend's hasty retreat as she hustled to the kitchen. "Scaredy cat," Millie muttered under her breath.

Millie headed in the opposite direction, towards Ocean Treasures, the gift shop where Catherine or "Cat" as her friends called her, worked. Of course, there was a good chance Millie was on the "persona non grata" list now, so it might be "Catherine" from here on out.

She smiled and nodded to a few of the crew as she passed them in the hall. Although Millie had only been working on the ship for a short time, the faces were beginning to look familiar.

Millie liked to pride herself on being able to remember details. Like so-and-so loved chocolate ice cream or that someone's mother was a school teacher in Little Rock or her ex-husband, Roger, refused to eat the food on his plate if his meat and vegetable touched each other.

Millie scowled at the thought of her cheating ex-husband. He picked the most inopportune times to invade her brain!

No, it was peoples' names that Millie had a hard time remembering.

Millie paused as she reached the outside corridor and the elevator. She could take the elevator but instead, headed for the stairs. It was good exercise and although there was no scale on board, except for the one in the gym, her clothes felt a little looser since she'd come on board, so the extra flights of stairs had helped shed the pounds.

Bright lights lit up the inside of Ocean Treasures gift shop. Millie grabbed the handle and twisted the knob. The door was locked.

Millie peeked around the edge of the doorframe and caught a glimpse of the top of

Cat's beehive hairdo as she bent over the display case near the rear of the store. Strands of hair stuck out all over her head. Gone was the smooth, sleek "do" that was Cat's signature style.

Millie gave the glass door two sharp raps and waited.

Cat's head popped up. Her green eyes narrowed when she saw Millie.

Millie mouthed the words, "Let me in."

In response, Cat shook her head. Her hand shot up and she gave Millie the middle finger. Millie could read her lips and what came out would make a sailor blush.

Millie was determined. She needed to talk to Cat, to explain her side of it. Cat needed to see that it wasn't really Millie's fault that Cat had been taken in for questioning in the death of Olivia LaShay, a ship employee and Cat's co-worker.

Millie crossed her arms, planted her feet in front of the door and defiantly stared at Cat. Cat tried her best to ignore Millie. It worked just fine until Millie moved in front of the large, plate glass window. She dropped to her knees, clasped her hands together and begged. "Will you puhleeze let me in?"

Cat rolled her eyes and headed to the front entrance. Millie thought she was going to unlock the door. Instead, she turned off the light and disappeared into the back storage room. She shut the door behind her.

Millie rose to her feet, wiped the dust from her knees and slowly shuffled away.

"Millie, do you copy?"

Andy, her boss, was calling her on the radio. She unclipped the radio and pressed the button. "I'm here."

"Passengers are starting to board," he told her.

Millie glanced at the stairs and then at the elevator. The elevator would be the quickest way down, but ever since the time Millie had been stuck in one and discovered she suffered from claustrophobia, she hated them.

Against her better judgment, she pressed the down button and hopped into the empty elevator. This particular elevator wasn't as bad as the others. The front was floor-to-ceiling glass and it faced the atrium area so Millie could see out.

She stepped inside and pressed the button. The elevator doors closed and it began its descent. The elevator was halfway down when it shuddered and then stopped. Millie could see they were halfway between floors.

Millie pressed the floor button again. The elevator made a small whirring noise but refused to budge. She pressed another button. Still nothing. Millie panicked and punched all the buttons.

The air inside the confined space was stifling. Millie's heart began to beat faster. She started to feel faint. She leaned forward and placed both hands on the rail, staring out at the atrium below.

It was as if the elevator was invisible. Millie waved her arms frantically. No one seemed to notice her. She reached back and pressed the emergency button. Nothing happened.

Millie sunk to her knees and peered out. Cat was walking by. Millie pounded on the glass. "Help! Help! I'm stuck inside," she yelled.

The movement caught Cat's attention. She stepped closer. Her eyes met Millie's. For a moment, Millie thought she was going to turn and walk away.

Cat glanced around the atrium. Over in the corner, two workers had removed a wall panel and were poking around at some electrical wires.

Millie watched as Cat tapped one of the men's shoulders and pointed at Millie. The man's eyes widened. He shook his partner's arm and the two of them stared at Millie, still kneeling on the floor of the elevator.

They raced across the open floor. One of them held up a finger as if to say, "One minute."

Millie pulled herself to her feet. She closed her eyes and thanked the Lord that someone was going to rescue her. Closing her eyes helped.

Millie forced herself to breathe in, breathe out. She continued the slow, rhythmic breathing until the elevator jolted and began to move.

The elevator reached the atrium floor and the doors sprung open. Millie sprinted out. Her eyes darted around the room as she searched for Cat but Cat, her rescuer, was long gone.

Chapter 2

Andy Walker, Cruise Director, was dressed in a crisp, white uniform and standing at attention when Millie sidled up. He glanced at his watch. "You're right on time, Mildred."

Millie frowned. No one ever called her Mildred, no one except her mother when she was growing up and only when she was angry.

"Did you see me? I was stuck in the elevator!" She pointed to the offensive object.

Andy shook his head. "No, I hadn't noticed." He seemed completely unconcerned that Millie could have easily been hurt. What if the thing had plunged to the bottom of the ship and she had died?

Dave Patterson, head of security, made a pass by. He gave Andy the thumbs up, which meant customs had cleared the ship and a fresh batch of passengers were now heading to the gangplank and would be boarding within minutes.

Andy cupped his hands to his mouth. "It's show time, everyone!" he shouted. The crew cheered – or maybe it was more like moaned. Millie couldn't be certain.

One of the crew swung the entrance door open and stood watching as other workers maneuvered the ramp, attaching it to the side of the ship.

Millie snorted. With the door open, she had a clear view of the ramp and the passengers that were winding their way up. It reminded Millie of a herd of cattle on stampede.

Andy raised an eyebrow. "What's so funny?"

Millie shrugged her shoulders. "Oh nothing." She wasn't sure if Andy would think her comparison was as humorous as she.

One of the most interesting parts of passengers boarding the ship was the hierarchy:

diamond passengers, the ones who had sailed the cruise line a bunch of times, boarded first.

After diamond were platinum guests and then gold. The last to board were the newbies - what cruise ship employees called "green legs" since they didn't have their sea legs yet.

Green legs were more apt to become seasick during rough seas, more likely to get a serious sunburn on the first day of the cruise when they laid out around the pool too long. Last but not least, they were more likely to throw caution to the wind, forget about their vacation budget and spend more money than they planned. The cruise line *loved* green legs almost as much as they loved diamond passengers.

Andy and his booming voice greeted guests. "Welcome aboard folks!"

The cattle gate was wide open and the guests began pouring in the atrium area. Millie spent the next several hours answering questions and directing guests to different areas of the ship.

She noticed that this week's cruise was full of large groups that boarded in clusters. Some of them looked to be college-age students.

Millie made a mental note to keep an eye on them. One group in particular started horsing around as soon as they boarded. Security had to step in and make their presence known, which seemed to settle the rowdy crowd down a bit.

By the time all the guests had boarded and security gave the all-clear to close the door and pull the ramp, Millie's feet were aching and her stomach grumbling. All she had time to eat was a quick breakfast of cold, rubbery eggs and dry toast.

She glanced at the ship's clock on the wall. It was already 4:30. Andy read her mind. "I'm sure you're starving. Go take a break, grab a bite to eat and head out to the lido deck to check on the guests while you're up there."

Millie nodded. She had stopped by the kitchen to see her friend, Annette, when she had

taken a brief break and Annette had told her that
one of her favorite dishes, meatloaf, was on the
menu. Millie was craving comfort food, good
old-fashioned meatloaf!

There was no line at the buffet. The eatery
was getting ready to close in preparation for the
dinner hour. Most of the guests had already
eaten and were up on lido getting ready sail
away.

Millie's roommate, Sarah, was behind the
counter, packing things up. She glanced up when
she spied Millie. "Where've you been all day?"

"Greeting guests." She grabbed a dinner plate
and tray and hurried down the line.

Sarah followed along on the other side. "I
heard you and Cat had a falling out."

Millie flinched. "Yeah, she's mad at me." It
never ceased to amaze her how fast news traveled
on the ship. She finished loading her plate and
headed to the table.

Millie ate her food alone and watched the passengers wander through the dining room as they explored the other side of the ship. She loved to watch the excited faces and the couples who seemed so happy together.

Her smile disappeared as she thought about her ex-husband, Roger, and how much fun they had had on their one and only cruise. Of course, that was before he ran off with one of his clients, Delilah Osborne, Millie's former friend and hairdresser.

Millie pushed the half-eaten plate of food away. She had lost her appetite, even though the meatloaf was delicious. For some reason, she decided now was a good time to have a pity party for herself.

She stacked her dishes on the tray and slid out of the seat. Millie dumped the uneaten food in the trash and wandered through the sliding glass doors and onto the lido deck. The deck party was in full swing.

Millie circled the lower level, gauging the burn level on several of the guests sprawled out in the lounge chairs that surrounded the pool.

Zack, one of the dancers on board and one of Millie's favorite staff, was leading a group of passengers in a lively rendition of the Electric Slide.

The ship had departed a bit behind schedule and the sun was already setting. Millie slid her sunglasses on and gazed out at the sea. The sunset was spectacular. The clouds floated along, high above, laced in shades of pink and blue, as they dotted the sky.

The ship had already passed South Beach and the shoreline was a speck in the distance.

Satisfied the party was going off without a hitch, Millie shuffled to the side stairs. It was time to head to the theater to check on the progress of the "Welcome Aboard" show, scheduled for later that evening.

She made it as far as the rear of the upper deck when three ear-piercing blasts sounded. Millie nearly jumped out of her skin! Seconds later, a nearby speaker came to life. "M-O-B portside. I repeat M-O-B portside!" The voice sounded a bit panicked and Millie could have sworn the voice belonged to Andy!

The radio attached to her hip crackled as a sea of voices shouted across the airwaves. From what she could make out – which wasn't much since half of what was being said was in English and the other in foreign languages - it sounded as if they were saying someone had gone overboard.

The ship slowed, it shuddered slightly, stopped and then started to turn.

Not far from where Millie was standing, a crowd began to gather one floor up and over to the portside. At least Millie assumed it was the portside. She hadn't quite gotten the ship lingo and her sense of direction wasn't that great.

She raced across the deck and darted up the steps, taking them two at a time. Millie rounded the corner of the spa deck. A group of people stood off in the corner near the VIP section, which was a section reserved for the diamond and platinum members. An area that was only accessible via a special room key.

The access door was wide open as throngs of people lined the rail and peered down at the deep, blue ocean. Millie joined them as she stood near the rail and looked over the side. Her detective radar went up as she tried to hear what the guests around her were saying.

The woman to the left of Millie lowered her voice and turned her head toward the man on the other side. "I hope they find Kyle."

The man next to her nodded. "Yeah, this is crazy. One minute Kyle is partying down and the next, he's gone overboard."

The woman lowered her voice. "You don't think..."

Dave Patterson, the ship's head of security, appeared on the scene. His eyes met Millie's as he walked past her and over to a woman who was wailing loudly.

A movement in the water caught Millie's eye. One of the lifeboats was circling the water. Millie pulled her cell phone from her pocket. She turned the phone on and switched it to camera-mode. As inconspicuously as possible, she began to take several photos of the crowd - the witnesses.

Millie snapped a picture of the young couple that had been talking. She hurried up and snapped a few more quick photos before sliding the phone back into her pocket.

Millie spied a small opening next to another couple on the scene. She squeezed in. "I heard a bloodcurdling scream. Next thing I know, the woman was trying to climb over the railing. Thank goodness a man a few feet away realized what she was about to do so he darted over, grabbed her and pulled her off the railing. I think she was going to jump!"

Millie's eyes widened. This sounded like a double suicide attempt – or maybe a murder / suicide!

Millie peered over the edge. The lifeboat had come to a stop. One of the crew, wearing a fluorescent yellow life jacket, dove into the water. He swam out a short distance and grabbed something. Someone was in the water!

The rescuer wrapped his arm around the person who was floating face down. Using his free arm, he swam back to the rescue boat where two men pulled them from the water. They disappeared below deck and out of sight.

A loud cheer went up from the spectators as the small rescue boat sped back to the ship. Millie was torn. *Should she run down to watch the crew bring the passenger back on board or stay put to see if she could glean any more information out of the people still hanging around*? She opted to hang tight. She was glad she did.

Dave Patterson led the hysterical young woman away. There was another man with Patterson. He looked vaguely familiar. He nodded at Millie as he passed by. She glanced at his nametag: *Juan Carlos*.

There was an empty spot where the woman and Juan Carlos had stood. Millie shuffled over to the open spot and leaned against the rail. The crew had secured the smaller boat and a large pulley began to lift the small boat back up to an empty spot between other emergency lifeboats.

The area was clearing out. Only a handful of passengers lingered near the edge of the railing. Millie scooted closer to a man who was waving his arms in the air.

She leaned in for a listen. "...and then I saw the woman shove something inside her beach bag. What was odd about it was she seemed downright calm. Seconds later, she began to scream and wail, as if...well, as if someone she loved had just gone overboard."

Millie raised her eyebrows. *What could be more important than getting help for your loved one or for anyone for that matter - who had just fallen more than 14 stories off the side of a cruise ship?*

She reached in her pocket and plucked out her cell phone. Millie snapped several more pictures of the area – including the man who had been talking.

Millie glanced down at her watch. With all the excitement, she had lost track of time. She was late for work!

Millie picked up the pace as she scrambled down several flights of stairs and bolted across the Atlantic deck to the theater.

The theater was dark except for a dim light that beamed out from under the red velvet curtain. Millie almost tripped over herself as she hurried around the seating and up the steps.

The performers were in the back make-up area, preparing for the show. Her eyes scanned the crowded room as she searched for Andy. He was nowhere in sight.

One of the dancers, Alison, caught her eye. She sauntered over. "Looking for Andy?"

Millie nodded.

Alison tugged on the edge of her sequined skirt. "He's down handling the man overboard crisis," she explained.

Millie let out the breath she'd been holding. Of course Andy would be there – which would give her the perfect excuse to check it out herself!

"Where are they?"

Alison looked around. "Down in medical." she leaned in. "I heard the guy was DOA."

"You mean the passenger is dead?" This was not good. Not good at all. The ship hadn't left port more than a couple hours ago and they already had a fatality. "Are we turning back?"

Alison shook her head. "You would think so but the suits said no. We continue on."

Millie thanked her and made her way back out of the theater. It was time to head to medical.

Chapter 3

Security was tight outside the medical center and Doctor Gundervan's office. Two guards nodded to Millie as she squeezed past the growing crowd and made her way inside.

The front waiting room was empty. Millie could hear voices coming from the back. The sound of a woman's sobs filled the air.

Millie stepped around the corner and her heart sank. The poor young woman she had seen up on deck was in a chair, hunched over, her face buried in her hands.

Andy stood nearby. He patted her shoulder soothingly. He gave Millie a quick look before leaning close to the woman. He whispered in her ear.

Captain Niccolo Armati was there, too. He was off in the corner speaking to Dave Patterson, the head of security on board the ship. Captain

Armati glanced in Millie's direction. His look was unreadable, his eyes dark.

Millie shivered. For some reason, she got the distinct impression that he did not care for her. She wasn't sure why, though. She'd only met him once and seen him around ship here and there. It wasn't like she had done anything wrong. At least not that she could think of.

She eased over to Andy's side. "You might have to do introductions for the Welcome Aboard show tonight," he muttered from the corner of his mouth. He gave her a hard stare. "You can do it, Millie."

A lump lodged in Millie's throat. She had only been on stage – in front of thousands of people – once, and Andy had been up there with her. Now he was telling her she had to take over and open the show.

What if she choked? Or worse yet – fainted? How embarrassing would that be?

The distraught woman began to cry again. A wave of guilt washed over Millie. Her biggest worry was stage fright. This poor woman had just lost a loved one! She stiffened her back and gave Andy a small salute. "Yes, sir. I'll get the job done," she assured him. If only she felt as confident!

Millie wandered out of the room and wound her way through the growing crowd. She wondered where they kept the bodies on board a ship.

She didn't have to wonder long as she watched two men, dressed in black, push a gurney through an open door. On top of the gurney was a white sheet that covered what Millie could only guess was a body.

Standing near the outer fringes of the crowd were Cat and Annette. They motioned her over to the other side of the corridor, out of earshot of the passengers.

Millie cautiously approached. She eyed Cat warily. "Thanks for rescuing me when I was trapped in the elevator," she said.

Cat gave a half shrug. "I can't stay mad. Annette explained your side of it and it wasn't really your fault I ended up in jail," she admitted.

Millie took a step closer. "Well, I want you to know that I'm really, really sorry," she said sincerely. "Truce?" She extended her hand.

Cat put her hand in Millie's hand. "Truce."

"Kiss and make up later," Annette interrupted. "So what happened?"

Millie told them everything she knew, including what she'd overheard from the witnesses. She patted her pocket. "I took pictures."

Cat's green eyes gleamed with interest. "Sounds like a new mystery to me!"

Annette faced Millie. "Cat would make a nice addition to our team."

Millie nodded. Cat would make a good addition. She had access to most of the passengers. A lot more than Annette, who was stuck in the kitchen most of the time.

Annette lowered her voice. "We need to have a little pow-wow after we're off duty. You know, go over everything and take a look at Millie's pictures."

The girls agreed to rendezvous at midnight in the library. Because Millie was assistant cruise director, she had access to areas of the ship that other staff and crew did not, including the library after hours.

Millie's heart was racing as she headed up the stairs and to the theater. She wasn't sure if it was the new mystery that was causing it – or the fact that soon she'd have to face thousands of guests on stage!

Zack waved his hand in the air, dismissing Millie's rapidly growing fears. "Millie, you'll be fine. You're a born natural," he told her.

Millie frowned. *She was a born natural, all right, but at what? That was the real question.*

Millie chewed her bottom lip. "What if I pass out on stage?"

"Just pretend that all of the passengers are naked," Zack suggested.

Millie sucked in a huge breath and pulled back the velvet curtain. She took a small step and then she froze in her tracks, unable to move forward. Suddenly, she felt a hard shove in the middle of her back.

Zack was pushing her! Millie half-stumbled, half-stepped out onto the stage. The lights were bright, almost blinding and it made it hard to see how many people were in the audience, which was probably a good thing. She couldn't see the crowd but she could sure hear them. Like the sound of a roaring sea. A sea of people. The place was packed!

Millie had heard Andy's Welcome Aboard presentation exactly one other time. Millie turned the microphone on and lifted it to her mouth. She pasted a smile across her face and started to talk about whatever came to mind, making it up as she went along.

Millie had always been fly-by-the-seat-of-your-pants kinda gal and tonight it worked for her.

By the time her bit was over and she had introduced the singers and dancers, she walked across the stage: floated, really. She was smiling and this time it was genuine.

Zack winked at Millie as he passed her on his way out. She gave him a grateful grin. If not for his encouragement, she might not have done it. Of course, the shove probably hadn't hurt, either.

When she hit the edge of the curtains, she ran smack dab into Andy, who was still applauding. "Bravo, my dear! That was fabulous!"

Millie handed him the mike as she stepped off the stage. The bright lights! The adoring crowds! Millie was on Cloud 9.

Andy studied her glow. "Uh-oh. I better watch out for Millie, the next cruise director of Siren of the Seas," he teased.

Andy was a great boss and a great guy. He was from across the pond and she loved his British accent and his polite manners, something that was greatly lacking in today's world. The fact that he had given her the opportunity to work side-by-side and learn from him made her appreciate her boss even more.

Andy lowered his voice. "The passenger that went overboard. He died." Millie nodded. She knew she needed to start her investigation promptly. The more time that passed, the less the witnesses would remember.

Andy went on to say that the girlfriend, Courtney Earhart, would disembark and return home tomorrow during the ship's first stop in Nassau in the morning.

Millie patted her pocket and her cell phone. She and the girls would study the pictures later, try to get near the passengers who had witnessed the horrific fall – or happened to be at the scene of the accident.

First on her list was to get as close as possible to Courtney Earhart, or her friends, to see what she could find out.

Andy set his mouth in a grim line as he watched the dancers shimmy and shake on stage. Overboards were the worst, in his opinion. An expert in cruise ship mishaps had come aboard for a talk with the entire crew and staff not long ago. He described all the various scenarios for accidents on board a cruise ship. He also gave them the warning signs to watch for.

The expert described what falling off the side of a cruise ship would feel like and it wasn't pretty. Depending on how the person hit the water, it would feel something akin to crashing onto a cement sidewalk at a horrific speed. "The young woman that was with him. His girlfriend is already talking about suing," Andy told her.

Andy turned his attention from the stage to Millie. His eyes narrowed. "I don't suppose you happened to..."

Millie finished his sentence. "...be up on deck right after it happened?" She patted her phone inside her pocket. "As a matter of fact, I was up on the lido, checking on the sail away party, which you told me to do," she reminded him.

Andy grinned. "Good girl. And?"

"Well. When I heard the horn blast and the 'MOB' crackle over the speaker, I knew something had happened. I saw a crowd gathering up in the VIP area so I headed that way."

Andy crossed his arms. He rocked back on his heels. "Go on."

"So I weaseled my way into the thick of things. You know, it's easier to put your ear to the ground so-to-speak if you're close by. I overheard a couple talking about a young woman and the man that went overboard."

Andy stopped her. "You don't happen to remember what they looked like?"

Millie reached into her pocket and pulled her cellphone out. "It's all right here. In case they needed to be questioned or what-not."

She handed the phone to Andy. He studied the first photo and swiped the screen to the next. There were several different shots. Millie had been thorough. She had snapped photos of the witnesses, the young woman. She even had a clear picture of the rescue boat in the water.

He stopped on the last frame. He frowned at the screen. His head shot up. "What was Zack Smythe doing up on deck? He was supposed to be back here practicing for tonight's show!"

Chapter 4

Millie grabbed the phone from Andy. She slipped her reading glasses on and stared down at the screen. Sure enough, right there, front and center, was Zack! What in the world was he doing up there? Andy was right. He should've been back stage practicing! Why hadn't Millie noticed him when she was up there? Here she thought she was honing her sleuthing skills and now this!

Millie scrolled through the rest of the pictures, looking for other familiar faces. There were two other staff and crew but she didn't recognize them right off the bat.

"I never noticed Zack up on the deck. Of course, there was a lot going on."

She could tell by the look on Andy's face he was going to have a chat with Zack. She touched his arm. "Maybe you should wait until the show is over. It might throw him off during the performance," she pointed out.

The singers and dancers were gearing up for the grand finale, which was right after the comedian finished his routine. If Andy and Zack got into it – it might throw not only Zack off, but anyone else within earshot. "You're right," Andy agreed. "I'll wait until it's over."

Millie watched as Andy headed to the dressing room to wait for the end of the show. She wanted to be anywhere but here. She wished the floor would open up and swallow her! Zack was her friend, and now he would think she had set him up. But she hadn't meant to! She hadn't even known he was up there!

This sleuthing thing was a tough business. First Cat and now Zack! By the time she was done, she wouldn't have any friends left! She would be public enemy #1!

Her shoulders drooped. She picked up her radio, trudged down the stairs and out of the theater. There was nothing left to do but wait for the chips to fall as they may – right on top of Millie's head!

Back in the lobby, Millie glanced down at her watch. She really needed one with glow in the dark hands so she could read it. In dark theaters, during stakeouts and hunting down criminals.

Andy had mentioned that the man overboard was a 25-year old American by the name of Kyle Zondervan. He was on the cruise with his 24-year old fiancé, Courtney. The couple had boarded with friends.

Millie reached for her cell phone and studied the pictures. She was certain the one set of witnesses were friends, the ones who mentioned Kyle by name.

Maybe they could shed some light on what might have been going on in the mind of young Kyle. Millie had heard the stories of folks who drank a bit too much on board and either jumped from the ship or pushed overboard by someone else in the heat of an argument.

She shuddered as she thought about what must have gone through the young man's mind on his way down, before he hit the water. Her stomach churned as she wondered if he felt anything.

She thought about her own children, just a few years older than Kyle and her heart went out to the family. Did they even know? Millie sent up a small prayer for his parents and family – and his fiancé.

She closed her eyes as she tried to memorize some of the faces. She still had an hour before she met Cat and Annette in front of the library.

She wandered past the shops and casino toward the other end of the ship. She passed the piano bar. The sound of music drifted from the open door. Guests were inside the bar singing: loud and off-key. Millie stepped inside the open

41

door. The bar was packed. Judging from the looks on the faces, the crowd was having fun.

She scanned the room. None of the faces looked familiar. She slowly backed out of the room.

Her next stop was the Tahitian Nights Dance Club. She could feel the music as it shook the floor beneath her. Millie opened the door and stepped inside. She spied the bartender, Robert, in the back of the bar. He gave Millie a quick nod as he poured a drink for one of the passengers.

Millie studied the crowd as she wandered over to a nearby stool and hopped up. He grabbed a towel, wiped his hands and stepped over. "Hey Millie...what'll you have? The usual?"

Millie raised a brow. She was impressed that she'd only been in the bar once or twice and he remembered her name. Did he actually remember what she drank? There was only one way to find out. "Sure. Thanks, Robert."

Robert grabbed a clean glass from under the counter and filled it with ice. He reached inside the cooler and pulled out a can of Diet Coke. He popped the top and poured the glass full before sliding it in front of her.

She plucked a straw from a nearby container and tore the wrapper off. "How do you do that?"

"What? Remember names or remember drinks?"

"Both." Maybe he could give her a few pointers.

He tapped the side of his forehead and smiled. "Sharp as a tack. I have a photographic memory. Mind like a steel trap." He rubbed an imaginary mark off the counter with the towel. "That and you're wearing a nametag *and* I can count on one hand how many people come into this bar and order a Diet Coke."

He wiped away a small puddle of water. "You hear about the MO?"

"You mean man overboard? The young man that went over?"

Robert tipped his head and nodded toward a dark corner. "Yeah. The girlfriend and some of her friends are over there."

Millie followed his gaze. A cluster of people huddled around a table near the back of the nightclub. She watched one of the girls in the middle of the fray down a shot. "Is that her?"

Robert nodded his head. "Yep. She's had..." He looked up for a magical number written on the ceiling. "Oh, at least four of those."

"What are they?" Millie was curious. She knew nothing about shots. Only that they were popular with the younger crowd. At least, that's what her children told her.

"Fireballs. They taste like cinnamon candy," he explained.

The small group began laughing loudly. The laughter echoed above the pulsing beat of the music. "I hope they don't get out of hand."

Robert smiled. "That's what old Brody is for."

"Who is Brody?"

"My unofficial bouncer." Robert pointed. "There he is now."

A burly man sporting a crew cut lumbered through the double doors. He reminded Millie of a wrestler. Or a marine. Either way, he was a big dude. One that Millie wouldn't want to mess with.

He stepped over to the counter and grunted at Millie. He glanced at her tag. "Who are you?" Apparently, pleasantries were not his strong suit. Millie scrunched up her nose. "Millie Sanders."

He nodded. "Huh." Then the light bulb went off in his head. "Hey, you're that nosy new assistant CD."

Millie sipped her Diet Coke. "That's me." Her reputation preceded her.

Robert poured a Sprite and set the glass in front of Brutus...err...Brody. He sucked the drink down in one long gulp and slammed the empty glass on the counter.

Robert poured another. This time, Brody took his time and downed only half the glass. "Always loved me a good mystery."

This was taking an interesting turn. Bouncer turned detective. Maybe he was an ex-cop. Brody leaned his elbow on the bar top and studied Millie. "What do you think of the guy who went over?"

Millie twisted her drink straw. "Not sure yet. I need to talk to a few witnesses. Talk to the deceased's family. You know, kind of see what was going on."

"Huh." Apparently, that was one of Brody's favorite words: *huh.*

He finished the rest of his drink and took a step back. "Let me know if you need any help on this one. Heard you're pretty good at figuring stuff out."

Millie thanked him and filed his name in the "he might be useful" category. One could never have too many people on your side, especially one Brody's size.

Millie slid off the barstool. "I better head out." Her eyes wandered to the corner crowd. The pitch was rising, just a bit higher. "Brody may want to stick around."

Robert nodded. "That's why he's here. He usually rolls in around 11:30 – 11:45 when the drinks start kickin' in."

Millie glanced down at her watch. It was time to meet the girls.

By the time Millie made it to the library, Cat and Annette were already waiting outside.

Millie had passed by the library a bunch of times but had never gone inside. It was cozy and inviting.

Millie loved libraries – and books. They took her to so many places. Places she'd never been. Of course, now she was actually going to some of the places she had only read about in her books!

Millie used her keycard to unlock the door. She pushed it open and stepped inside. Cat and Annette trailed behind.

The girls headed to a section behind the center bookshelf, out of sight of people passing by.

Annette grabbed a pad of paper and small pencil from a basket nearby. She rolled up her sleeves and plopped down. "Well, what've you got?"

Millie turned her phone on. She scrolled to the pictures and handed the phone to Annette. "I took these earlier when I was up on deck; right after the poor young man went over."

48

Annette grabbed the phone and stared down at the screen. "Heard his fiancé is getting off in Nassau in the morning." She passed the phone to Cat.

Millie had heard the same thing. She wished she had a chance to somehow get close to Courtney Earhart, maybe talk to her. Get a feel for what she was thinking. Find out if she knew anyone who had motive. Of course, it was quite possible that she herself had done him in. She certainly had the opportunity.

The girls studied the pictures while Millie told them what she had overhead. "So we need to talk to the people that saw the couple just moments before the unfortunate incident."

Cat tapped a long, perfectly manicured red nail on the table. "Let me see the pictures again."

Millie turned the phone and tapped the screen. She handed the phone to Cat.

Cat pointed to the couple Millie had overhead. "I think I saw them in the gift shop earlier," she told them. "They were buying – uh - ."

"Well?" Annette prompted. "What were they buying?"

Cat averted her eyes. "Personal protection supplies."

Millie shook her head. "Flashlights and nightlights?"

"No." Cat rolled her eyes. "C-o-n-t-r-a-c-e-p-t..."

Millie held up a hand. "Oh! Gotcha!"

"Anyways. We don't sell too many of those. I mean, most people bring their own. That's why I remember it."

"Can't be that unusual," Annette chimed in. "After all, in the rush to pack I've forgotten my toothbrush before."

Cat shrugged. "Either way, I can count on one hand how many of those personal products the ship sells. At least by me," she added. She nodded to the phone. "Now that I have the faces, I'll see what I can find out next time they come into the store."

"You mean you think they'll come back to buy more? How much of that stuff do you need for just one week?" Annette was stunned.

Cat shook her head. "No! No, I mean if they come in to buy souvenirs and such!"

"Good plan." Millie could see that Cat would be a valuable member of their little detective team. She had the most contact with passengers, other than Millie herself, of course.

"What can I do?" Annette wondered.

Millie didn't have a good plan for her. Not yet. "I'll have to get back with you."

Although Millie didn't have an assignment for Annette, but she did have a plan for herself.

Head back to the scene of the incident, and there was no time like the present!

Chapter 5

The spa deck was empty. Millie took the steps two at a time, passing by the deserted VIP area on her way. She shivered in the damp evening air. It was a bit creepy being up there all alone, knowing that only hours earlier a young man's last few moments on earth had been spent right here.

She wandered over to the railing and rested her elbows on the top rail. The ocean below was dark – almost black. Black like death. She stared at the waves, wondering how many people were lost at sea each year. How many dead bodies were at the bottom of the ocean.

Her mind took a dark turn. Maybe sharks or other sea creatures ate them. Millie shook her head to clear it.

She needed to focus. Millie forced herself to study the area. It wasn't large. Only enough room for maybe a dozen people if they were crammed in kind of tight. No. This area was more for intimate moments - for couples.

She studied the railing. It was high. Too high for someone to accidentally "fall" off. One would either have to climb up on the rail and jump or perhaps taken off guard and pushed.

She wandered along the sides and took one last look at the water before turning to go. She took a step down and stopped. Someone was coming up. Millie backed up. *Who would be coming up here this late at night?* She wondered.

She melted into the shadows, listening to the light "tap, tap" as someone made their way up the stairs. The little bit of light from the moon outlined a silhouette. It was a woman. The figure swayed when it got to the top step, reaching out to grab the handrail as the person fought to regain their balance.

When the woman took a step closer, into the light, Millie's eyes widened. It was the girl – the fiancé! She was alone. The woman teetered back and forth, as she stumbled forward and almost fell.

Millie caught a whiff of cinnamon. She was certain the young woman was drunk!

She didn't notice Millie as she staggered toward the railing. Her back was to Millie now.

Millie watched as the young woman leaned over the rail and heaved, which made Millie's own stomach wrench. Millie had a bit of a weak stomach and watching someone vomit made her want to hurl. The sight of blood did, too.

Millie cleared her throat. The girl spun around. Well, not really spun. More like drifted to the side while still gripping the handrail. "Wh- Who're you?"

"Millie, the assistant cruise director," Millie replied. "Are you alright?" She glanced down at the young woman's silky blue summer dress and the fresh stains now darkening the front.

Millie swallowed hard and tried to focus on the girl – not the vomit.

"My bo-frend. Uh, I mean fe-ance." Courtney hiccupped and wiped her mouth with the back of her hand. "He drown." She began to cry. Huge, gulping sobs wracked her body.

Millie's heart wrenched. She stepped closer. She leaned forward and wrapped an arm around her shoulder, careful to steer clear of the stains. "I'm sorry to hear that, dear." She patted her back, not sure what else she could say that would help.

The girl dropped her head on Millie's shoulder. Tears soaked Millie's shirt, dampening her skin. She wished she had a Kleenex, something she could hand the poor thing.

Courtney hiccupped again. She raised a tear stained face and looked into Millie's eyes. "He dint kill himself." She swayed ever-so-slightly. Millie reached out to hold her steady. "Sum-sum body PUSHED him over."

She stumbled back and pointed a crooked finger to the water. "I went to the baf-room and when – when I came back, he was gone." She stared out at the black water. "I heard him scream just before he hit the water."

She swayed back around to face Millie. She leaned in so close; her forehead almost touched Millie's. Her big blue eyes, pupils dilated, bore holes. "What if I'm nex?"

Millie put both hands on her shoulders to stop her from pulling both of them to the ground. "Why would you think you're next?"

"Cuz they tole Kyle he was gonna die." She slapped her hand over her mouth and stumbled to the railing where she threw up again. Millie looked away but she could still hear it. She wasn't sure what was worse – seeing someone toss their cookies – or hearing it.

She clenched her own stomach and willed the churning to stop.

Courtney was done. She wiped her mouth on the top of her dress, which now had even more stains.

"Who told Kyle he was gonna die?" Millie asked.

Courtney shook her head. "I better not say." Her eyes darted around the deck. She waved her hand. "I'm leeveng ina mor-morning. I should go pack."

The poor girl was so drunk she could barely stand. "Let me help you back to your cabin," Millie offered.

Courtney nodded. "Yur a nice lay-dee." Her head rolled forward. She squinted at Millie's tag. "Whas your name?"

"Millie."

Millie helped Courtney down the steps and it was a good thing. There were a few times that Courtney almost tripped both of them. Millie nearly lost her hold and they lurched forward.

"What's your cabin number?"

Courtney lifted a hand. She extended her index finger and began to count. Her eyebrows furrowed as she stared at her wavering finger. "One. Two. Three. Four." Her knees started to give out. Millie wedged her shoulder under Courtney's arm in an effort to keep her upright.

"I'm in forty-two, ohhhhh. Four!" Courtney smiled, proud that she remembered her cabin number.

Millie headed for the nearest bank of elevators, half-dragging, half-carrying young Courtney. They were halfway home! Millie jabbed the down button and waited. When the door opened, Millie sent up a small prayer, thankful that no one was inside to witness the scene.

Millie forced herself not to focus on her recent run in with the elevator in the atrium as the women stumbled inside. Millie pressed the close button.

It took all of Millie's strength to keep Courtney from sinking to the floor. When the doors opened, the two of them stumbled out and into the hall.

They wandered down the long hall to the aft of the ship.

Courtney pulled her key card from the top pocket of her dress and dropped it into Millie's open hand. Millie slid the card into the slot and pushed the door open.

The room was lit up like a Christmas tree. Every single light in the entire place was on.

"'fraid of the dark," Courtney mumbled. Millie couldn't blame her. Especially considering her fiancé had just died and now the girl thought someone was out to get her.

The girls half-stepped, half-stumbled across the threshold. Millie helped guide her across the short distance and over to the bed. Courtney fell forward, face down on the bed, and then lay motionless. She was so still, Millie wondered if she was still alive.

She leaned forward and studied the still figure. She let out the breath she'd been holding when she saw Courtney's chest rise, ever-so-slightly.

Millie gently shook her shoulder. "Courtney." No response. She leaned closer. "Courtney!" Still nothing. The girl was out cold.

Millie grasped her shoulder and gently rolled her to the side. At least if she was on her side and she threw up again, she wouldn't suffocate, Millie reasoned.

Millie grabbed the pillows from the bed and propped them up and around her to keep her in place.

Millie straightened. She stuck a hand on her hip and studied the young woman's still form. Satisfied Courtney wasn't going anywhere anytime soon, she offered up a quick prayer.

Millie placed the young woman's key card on the dresser and slipped out the door, tugging on it to make sure it locked behind her.

It was late. Millie was exhausted. Turnover day had taken a turn for the worse. As she crawled into bed, she had a bad feeling that tomorrow wasn't going to be much better.

Millie prayed for Kyle, the young man who had lost his life, and his family. It was hard to imagine the heartbreak his family was going through right now. She also prayed for young Courtney. The poor thing had some rough days ahead of her.

As soon as Millie unclasped her hands, they fell to her side and she was out, not unlike poor Courtney.

Chapter 6

Millie was dreaming. In her dream, she was running across the lido deck. Someone was chasing her. She picked up the pace and began to run.

Millie cast a furtive glance over her shoulder. The person chasing her was dark and menacing.

Millie was certain it was a man and he was closing in on her! Millie tried to run faster, but the faster she ran, the closer he got.

She made it to the steps, grabbed the handrails and raced down the steps. Her feet thumped loudly on the stair treads.

Icy fingers touched the back of her bare neck. Millie shivered at the touch.

She closed her eyes and the thumping came again. Except it was louder and this time it wasn't a dream!

Her eyes flew open. She was awake now and someone was pounding on the cabin door.

Millie flung back the covers. Her feet dropped to the floor and she shuffled over to the door, opening it just far enough to peek out through the crack.

It was Andy. The first thing she noticed was his typically clean-shaven face had day old stubble. The second thing she noticed was that he was wearing the same outfit he'd had on the day before. It was almost as if he hadn't gone to bed yet.

Millie grabbed his hand and pulled him inside. She shut the door behind them. "Are you okay?"

Andy leaned his head back against the wall and shut his eyes. "She's dead."

"Who is dead?"

"The girl, Courtney Earhart. They found her body a short time ago." Andy rubbed his temple. "The room steward knocked on the door and when she didn't answer, he let himself in to make up the bed and clean the cabin."

Millie swallowed hard. "H-how did she die?" She hoped the poor thing hadn't somehow managed to roll over and suffocate herself. If that were the case, Millie would never be able to forgive herself.

She knew she should have stayed with her, waited until she was semi-sober before leaving. Millie had been 100% certain the girl was out for the night; convinced that she would probably wake up with a killer hangover but at least she would wake up. This didn't seem to be the case now.

Andy rubbed the stubble on his chin. "Overdose. She left a suicide note."

"Overdose?" Millie would have thought it would be alcohol poisoning.

Andy nodded. "Some sort of anti-depressant. They found the empty bottle next to her body."

Millie furrowed her brows. How could that be? Courtney wasn't even capable of walking to the bed by herself, let alone finding a bottle of prescription drugs and downing the whole thing. On top of that, she obviously had a weak stomach. Millie herself had been a witness to that. It was very odd. Something was not adding up.

"Where is she now?"

Andy shoved his hands in his pockets. "In the cooler, right next to her fiancé, Kyle."

"Cooler?"

"You know...the morgue."

If there was any comforting thought to the entire tragedy, it was that they were together now. "Can we make a run down to her room? You know, so I can take a peek?"

Millie held her breath. It didn't hurt to ask. She wasn't sure if Andy would agree or not.

"That's why I'm here. You have a nose for this stuff and now with two deaths in less than 24 hours, we're going to need all the help we can get."

Millie made a quick trip to the bathroom to change into street clothes before she grabbed her cell phone and followed Andy out of the cabin.

Millie mulled over the previous evening's events and her conversation with a very intoxicated Courtney. She remembered how Courtney had mentioned she thought Kyle had been murdered and alluded to the fact that she might be next.

She would tell Andy what had transpired the night before but not until she had a chance to look around the cabin for clues. "I have something to tell you, but want to wait until I look at the room."

He didn't have a chance to answer. They were standing outside the open cabin door. Two men, dressed in ship's security uniform, were inside. Millie tiptoed in, careful not to touch anything.

She plucked her cell phone from her front pocket and began snapping pictures. She took pictures of the bed, the floor. With the tip of her shoe, she eased the bathroom door open and took a couple quick photos.

The closet door behind her was ajar. She stuck her elbow in the gap and nudged the door open before snapping a few shots of the interior.

Satisfied that she had as many photos as she would possibly need, she turned to Andy. "Any chance I can take a peek in the you-know-what?" She jerked her head toward the hall.

He nodded and waved her out. They walked silently down the long hall. When they got to the stairs, they made their way down several flights and headed in the direction of the medical center.

They stopped at the end of a long hall, in front of a door marked, "Restricted Area." Andy pulled his key card from his pants pocket and inserted it in the slot.

Millie sucked in a breath. She wasn't used to looking at dead bodies. Only on TV. She hoped she wouldn't embarrass herself and pass out cold.

"...better to ask for forgiveness than ask for permission," Andy was saying.

"I'm sorry, Andy. I didn't catch all that."

"No. I was just saying I'm not sure if this is against policy, letting you back here and all. But that I'd rather ask for forgiveness than ask for permission."

Millie liked that saying. She'd have to remember that for future reference. If she overstepped her boundaries. Say, during an investigation.

She followed Andy into the small room. One bare bulb hung from the low ceiling. The room was cold and sterile. Millie shivered.

Over in the corner, pressed together against the far wall, were two gurneys. A white sheet covered each of the gurneys. The outline of bodies was clearly visible: the bodies of Kyle Zondervan and Courtney Earhart. "Are these being taken off today?"

Andy answered in a low voice, almost a whisper. "Yes, the authorities are waiting for customs to clear the ship."

He took a step closer. "You want to take a peek?"

Millie was torn. She did and she didn't. What if there was a clue, something that would help solve the murders...unless, of course, Courtney was responsible for their deaths.

No! Something in Millie's gut told her it wasn't that cut and dried. Determined to get to the bottom of it, she took a deep breath and nodded. "I'm ready."

Andy lowered the sheet that covered Kyle Zondervan's body first. Millie avoided looking at his face. He was dressed in khaki shorts and a pale green button down shirt. On his feet was a pair of tennis shoes.

She switched her phone to camera and took a quick snapshot. "Okay."

Andy carefully covered him back up and shifted to Courtney's body. Millie knew this one would be harder to see. He pulled the sheet back and once again, Millie avoided looking at her face. She took a couple quick photos. "That should be enough."

Andy pulled the sheet back over her body and they stepped from the room. "So what do you think?"

Millie looked up and down the corridor. There was a group of people further down the hall, out of earshot. Then she dropped the bombshell. "I met Courtney last night. She was up in the VIP area."

She went on to explain to Andy everything that had happened. How Courtney was so drunk, Millie helped her back to her room and that when they got there, the young woman had passed out on the bed. "She was out cold and that's why I'm not sure I believe that she committed suicide. I mean, she couldn't even stand up, let alone write a suicide note and then down a bunch of pills." She shook her head. "Something doesn't add up here."

Andy tugged on the edge of his ear. "They're comparing the handwriting on the note to the form that Courtney filled out the other day when she boarded."

The "form" was a form all passengers were required to fill out prior to boarding. It was a small questionnaire, really, where guests checked boxes and signed off saying they hadn't been exposed to certain illnesses and that they themselves had no flu-like symptoms.

"What about witnesses? Friends of the couple?" Millie remembered the previous night in the club when Courtney and her friends had been off in the corner drinking. Surely, someone would be able to shed some light on Courtney's state of mind and her relationship with Kyle. It would also be helpful to know whether or not it was on the rocks.

"They've been interviewed," Andy said. He looked down at his crumpled shirt and wrinkled slacks. "I have to go shower before guests are up and around. Can't have the cruise director looking like a train wreck."

The two wandered down the steps to "I-95," the main employee corridor and crew quarters. "I'll meet you up in my office in an hour." Millie nodded and watched as he disappeared down the hall and around the corner. She headed back to her cabin to go over what she had so far.

The cabin was empty when she got there. In fact, now that Millie thought about it, it was empty when Andy showed up on her doorstep earlier. Sarah, Millie's cabin mate, must have pulled an early shift.

Millie grabbed a clean uniform from the closet and slipped it on. She pulled out the only chair in the cabin and plopped down at the desk. With her glasses firmly on her nose, she scrolled through the photos of the VIP deck right after Kyle went overboard.

Somehow, she needed to talk to the friends of Courtney and Kyle, to see what their thoughts were. That was her first order of business.

When Millie got to the second picture, she noticed Zack, standing off to the side. He didn't look happy. *Why was he there? Had he just happened to be passing by and stumbled upon the accident after it happened?* Zack was next on her list.

She studied the photo of the suicide note.

74

Next, she focused on the picture of the cabin. It looked a lot like it had the previous night when Millie had helped Courtney to her room.

She flipped past the photo of the makeup counter, then scrolled back. She tapped the screen and zoomed in. The room card. The one that Millie had placed on the counter before leaving was in the exact spot that Millie had left it, which meant that Courtney never left the room after Millie.

There was something different about the photos. Something that Millie couldn't quite put her finger on. She'd have to think about it, but for now, she had to get going. It was time for work.

Chapter 7

Millie wandered into the backstage dressing room on her way to Andy's small office. Andy and Zack were standing in the far corner. Andy's face, red with frustration, was mere inches from Zack's face. Millie could hear every single word.

She scooched a little closer but still out of sight. Millie pretended to straighten some of the makeup cases and arrange the hairbrushes. "...and you should never have been up on deck. If anyone finds out you knew Courtney, dated her even, and that you were up on deck when her fiancé died, it is going to put you right in line for suspicion."

Millie's eyes widened. *Zack had dated the dead girl?* If that were true, he would most certainly be a suspect.

"But she asked me to come up there and talk to her," Zack argued.

"Why?"

Zack shrugged. "Never got a chance to ask. All I know is she was upset and I couldn't tell her no."

Millie slipped back around the corner before Zack or Andy spotted her.

She cleared her throat and entered the room. "Hey guys."

Andy stepped forward while Zack eased past Millie and hightailed out of the dressing room.

The two of them stepped into his small office, which was really just a partitioned cubby off in the corner. They went over the schedule for the next two days.

Millie wasn't surprise that he put her in charge of trivia again. She was surprised that he scheduled her to host bingo. On her own. She started to protest. Andy held up his hand. "You're good Millie. Don't sell yourself short."

"But…"

"No buts."

Millie closed her mouth and they continued going over the rest of the schedule.

After they finished, Millie headed to the kitchen to track down Annette. A lot had happened since the three women had met in the library.

Annette looked as if she were about to explode when she saw Millie saunter in. She grabbed her hand and pulled her to the corner, right next to the walk-in freezer. "The fiancé is dead," she hissed.

Millie nodded. "Andy told me."

"She left a suicide note."

"Andy told me that, too."

Annette stuck her hand on her hip. She tipped her head to the side. "Well, did he tell you the bodies are off the ship today but all the friends decided to stay on board?"

"No." Millie shook her head. She did not know that but she was glad they were staying on. Hopefully, she'd have a chance to track them down.

Annette glanced around. She lowered her voice. "Cat said the friends of the couple were in the store this morning. She said to stop by when we had time. She might have something."

That was promising. A lead! Millie turned to go. "I'll head up there now."

"Without me?" Annette seemed so disappointed; Millie relented and told her she would wait. That they would go together.

Millie left the kitchen promising Annette they'd run by there when she took her afternoon break at three. She had half an hour before the first round of trivia started. Millie decided it would be best to avoid the gift shop since it would be too tempting to swing on in there.

Instead, she decided to take a shortcut through the casino, which was directly across from the shops. She made a beeline down the center aisle when something – actually, someone – caught her attention.

There, sitting at a row of machines near the door, was the couple that had been on the deck when Kyle went overboard: Courtney and Kyle's friends. They were engrossed in play and didn't notice Millie as she slowed to a stroll and pretended to study the machines.

The girl picked up a half-empty beer bottle and took a sip.

The whole thing was a bit odd. The two of them didn't appear to be distraught over the sudden death of their supposed friends. Shouldn't they be a bit more somber, more subdued?

The guy leaned over and whispered something in the woman's ear. She laughed and went back to playing her machine. *With friends like that, who needs enemies?* Millie thought to herself.

The woman glanced up at Millie. Her eyes narrowed as they traveled up Millie's uniform and settled on her nametag. She grabbed her beer off the ledge and tapped the man's leg. "C'mon. Let's get out of here."

The two abruptly rose from their seats and exited the casino. Millie watched them as they headed to the elevators. Maybe they thought she was following them.

Millie shrugged and went in the opposite direction, toward the trivia area. She spent the next hour engaging a large group of passengers. This trivia contest was a bit different from the others she had hosted so far. Millie played clips of hit songs and the guests had to guess the artist and song name.

It was harder than it seemed and no one got them all right, although one couple came close. Millie was excited with the prize this time. It was a buy-one, get one-free coupon for bingo.

She was wrapping up the trivia, putting the folder in the cupboard and locking the door when Annette careened around the corner. "You didn't see Cat yet?"

"Nope." Millie shook her head. "We're going together, remember?"

The two women picked up the pace as they made their way into the gift shop. Cat was waiting on customers so Millie and Annette wandered around, inspecting the what-nots inside. After the customers left, Millie and Annette headed to the cash register near the back.

Cat skipped the small talk. "The couple came back in. You know, the specialty products purchasers."

She patted the top of her head, waved to someone through the plate glass window, then leaned forward. "They seemed pretty shook up about their friends."

The complete opposite of what Millie had just experienced. "Go on."

"Well, the girl had said Courtney was getting threatening notes and she felt like she was being stalked."

"And?"

"Well, I said. 'How can that be? You think someone on board the cruise ship was out to get them?'"

"Then the girl said that Zack. You know, Zack Smythe, had dated Courtney and had some sort of serious obsession with her."

Zack had been in the area when young Kyle went overboard. Was Zack there when Courtney died? He wouldn't have access to guests cabins, unlike Millie who had a master key. Of course,

Courtney could have let him in, let someone in her room that she knew.

Things were not looking good for Zack, at least not in Millie's opinion.

"So the couple are staying on? The friends?"

Cat grabbed a bottle of glass cleaner and sprayed the top of the counter. "That is one of the things I asked. You know, after all, it sounds like they were good friends and such."

Millie hoped they were staying. She was planning on the fact that they were staying. There was more to their story than they were letting on and Millie planned to get to the bottom of it.

Then Cat dropped a bombshell or, as Millie liked to describe it, another wrench into the mystery. "Yes. They're finishing the cruise. Not only them, but Kyle's ex-girlfriend, who also happens to be Courtney's sister."

Chapter 8

Millie shook her head as if to clear it. These young kids were beginning to sound like the old soap opera, "Peyton Place," where everyone seemed to be running around with everyone else.

Cat stuck her hand on her hip. Millie could tell she had something juicy to add. Probably another unexpected twist. "The girls – Courtney and her sister, Chloe, were identical twins. You know. They look, or looked, exactly alike."

Millie's forehead crinkled. This did add a new level of intrigue and mystery to the case. Zack had dated Courtney and he was at the scene of the first incident.

The friends didn't seem particularly shaken up by the murder/suicide of their close friends. On top of that, Courtney's twin sister, Chloe, was still on board the ship and she had dated her sister's fiance!

"You have any idea who the friends are? Do you know their names?"

Cat shook her head. "Nope. I tried to keep them in the store, make enough small talk where they mentioned it or even called each other by name but they never did."

"What about looking at their room cards when they – ahem – purchased their goods?" Annette asked.

Cat frowned. "I did glance at the card the woman handed me and I saw the name." She let out a sigh. "For the life of me, I just can't remember what it was."

Millie snapped her fingers. "I have an idea on how we can get their names."

Maybe Donovan Sweeney could help her. After all, he was the purser on board the ship. Didn't he have access to all the records of the passengers? She wasn't sure if it might be against company policy but at least it was worth a try!

Millie added it to her to-do list. First, she planned to make a run back to the dressing room to see if Zack was around.

Millie's heart sank when she spotted several of the dancers clustered in a small group in the dressing room back stage. Zack was right in the thick of it. He looked upset, his face flushed and swollen.

Millie thought he looked as if he might cry. When the others saw Millie coming, they stepped aside and busied themselves at their respective counters.

Zack didn't seem to have much luck keeping the women in his life alive. First Olivia LaShay had been murdered and now Courtney Earhart.

Millie made her way over to Zack, leaned forward and gave him a warm hug. A small sob escaped his lips.

"I can't believe she's gone." The words escaped Zack's lips in a low moan. "She didn't kill herself. I just know she didn't."

Millie didn't think so, either, considering the condition she had left her in.

She led Zack into Andy's small cubicle and motioned to the chair. She pulled a tissue from a nearby Kleenex box and handed it to him.

Zack wiped his eyes and loudly blew his nose. Millie eased into the chair next to him. "They're already questioning me as if I'm a suspect."

Millie wondered who "they" were.

"You know. Dave Patterson."

Millie nodded. That made sense, since Dave had been one of the first people on the scene when Kyle went overboard. On top of that, he was head of security.

"What do you think happened?" she asked.

"I don't think Courtney killed herself. I don't think she killed Kyle, either." He wadded the tissue in a ball. "Think about it. Kyle was way bigger than Courtney. Do you really think she would have the strength to push a big guy like him overboard?"

Millie wasn't sure how much she should be telling Zack, but she had to get his thoughts. After all, he knew Courtney better than most. "I met Courtney last night up near the scene of the accident. She was drunker than a skunk. She mentioned feeling threatened. It was almost as if she thought someone was trying to kill her. Kill them," Millie added.

Zack slowly nodded. "Courtney wanted to talk to me. She left me a message saying it was urgent. That's why I was up on deck, to try to track her down."

"What about her sister, Chloe?"

Zack shook his head. "I can't see Chloe as a killer but then you never know. She dated Kyle for about a year. When they broke up, Kyle started dating Courtney."

"How did Chloe feel about that?"

Zack shrugged. "How would anyone feel if you were madly in love with a guy and he broke up with you only to turn around and propose to your twin sister?"

That's what Millie suspected. A love triangle gone wrong, but to what level was the hurt and hate? Was it deep enough to kill someone? Millie was about to find out.

Zack extended his arm. "Chloe was so in love with Kyle, she had his name tattooed on her arm." He pointed to the inside of his arm, just above his elbow. It was in a place one would not be able to see unless the under arm was visible. "Right there."

"Is Chloe capable of murder?" He shrugged. "I don't know. All I do know is it wasn't me."

Millie wanted to believe him.

"Can you help me get out of this mess? Andy told me they might fire me if they can't clear my name soon."

Her heart sunk because she didn't want to see Zack go. He was one of her favorite staff on board. Always upbeat, trying to help Millie adjust, giving her tips, encouraging her, pushing her onto the stage when she froze...

She patted his hand. "I'll do whatever I can to get to the bottom of this," she promised him.

Millie got to her feet. "First, I need to talk to the friends. Do you know their names?"

Zack grabbed another tissue and dabbed at his eyes. "Adam and Melissa West."

That should make it easy for Donovan to find their room. She repeated the name in her head, hoping she wouldn't forget it!

She whispered it under her breath, all the way to the guest services desk. She must have looked a bit weird talking to herself as she walked. She did get a few odd stares, not that she minded. It was more important to remember the names than to worry about appearances.

Her eyes scanned the customer service desk. Donovan wasn't on duty. She grabbed a pad of paper and pencil to jot down a note. "I need to talk to you ASAP." She folded the message in half and stuffed it in Donovan's cubby.

Millie turned to go and ran smack dab into a woman that could have been Courtney Earhart's twin. It had to be her twin sister, Chloe!

Millie shifted to the side. Chloe stepped to the counter. The only other person working behind the counter was busy helping another passenger.

Millie seized her opportunity. "Can I help you with something?"

Chloe gave Millie a sideways glance. "I-I was gonna see if they might let me into my sister's cabin. Courtney Earhart." The girl pulled a card from her pocket. "Here. Here's my ID."

Millie glanced at the key card: *Chloe Earhart.*

Millie handed the card back and reached for the lanyard around her own neck - the one that gave her access to all areas of the ship, including passengers' cabins. "Is there something inside you need to get?"

Millie wasn't sure if they still considered Courtney and Kyle's cabin a crime scene and if it was off-limits. She was torn. She *could* open the door to Courtney's cabin. She could also get in a whole lot of hot water...probably. Of course, she could claim ignorance as a new employee.

Erring on the side of the investigation, Millie touched her arm. "I can let you in."

Chloe Earhart looked up. "You can?"

The women headed to the elevator. "The stairs will be quicker," Millie pointed out.

Chloe nodded. "Okay."

Questions were swirling 'round Millie's mind. Questions she was dying to ask. Like why would she stay on board and not get off with her sister's body, not to mention her ex-boyfriend's body?

Chloe clenched the handrail. "I know I should've gotten off. My parents. Well, they're devastated."

Chloe stopped abruptly. "My sister won't be laid to rest until I get back home. I'll get off this ship, but I'm not leaving until I get to the bottom of this and find Courtney's killer," she vowed, "and Kyle's."

Millie's eyes wandered down her arm in search of the tattoo that Zack had mentioned. The spot with Kyle's name. Unfortunately, Chloe was wearing long sleeves.

She followed Chloe down the steps to Deck 4. The same deck Millie had been on the night before when she helped Courtney to her cabin.

They stopped in front of cabin 4204. Courtney's cabin. Millie glanced down the long hall, took a deep breath, and lifted her lanyard from her neck. She pushed the key card in the slot. The lock clicked, Millie pushed the door open and followed Chloe Earhart inside.

Chloe spun around. She glanced down at Millie's tag. "You - you're..."

"Millie Sanders, the assistant cruise director."

Chloe nodded. "I ran into Zack Smythe earlier. Are you the one that helped Courtney to her cabin?"

Millie nodded.

"So you were the last person to see Court alive?"

Millie blinked. She had been the last person – which would make her a prime suspect. The thought hadn't occurred to her. Did that mean security would be coming to track her down and arrest her?

Chloe didn't wait for an answer. She opened the bathroom door, looked inside and closed it. She wandered around the room, as if looking for something.

"Is there something specific you needed, dear?"

Chloe looked at Millie then dropped her gaze to the floor. She shrugged. "I don't know. A clue maybe? Something the investigators might have missed?"

Millie didn't think that would be the case. After all, the room was small. It wouldn't take long to search every square inch of the cabin.

Still, Chloe seemed determined. She lifted the edge of the mattress.

Millie pulled open a closet door and peered inside the dark space. It was empty. She started to shut the door when something caught her eye. Something blue. Millie reached in and grabbed hold of a silk fabric.

She pulled it out and unfolded it, holding it up.

Chloe dropped the edge of the mattress and stepped closer. "What's that?"

Millie frowned. What it was - was the stained dress that Courtney Earhart had been wearing the night of her death.

Millie draped the dress over her arm. She slipped her cell phone from her pocket and turned it on. She scrolled to the pictures she had taken of Courtney in the morgue. She slipped her glasses on and pulled the phone close. Courtney was wearing a different dress - a pink one!

That meant that if Courtney committed suicide, she managed to change into a clean dress, write a suicide note and then overdose on a bunch of pills, all the while inebriated to the point of passing out. This scenario was highly unlikely.

Chloe pointed to the dress draped across Millie's arm. "This is the dress Courtney was wearing the last time I saw her alive!"

Millie turned the phone so Chloe could see the dress Courtney had on when security discovered her body. "Does this dress look familiar?"

Chloe's eyes grew wide. "That dress belongs to Melissa! I watched her unpack it and put it in her closet! I only know 'cuz I remember telling her how much I liked it."

Chloe lifted the stained dress from Millie's arm. She held it up. "Maybe you can talk to Adam and Melissa?"

Millie paused. Why would she talk to Adam and Melissa if she, Chloe, was bound and determined to get to the bottom of her sister's death?

"I could." She looked around. "I need to find out what cabin they're in."

"Well, that's easy," Chloe replied, "it's right next door!"

Millie's radio began to squawk. "Millie. Do you copy?" It was Andy. She glanced at her watch and discovered she was late! Ten minutes late to be precise. "I'm here, Andy. I'm on my way."

"Meet me in front of the watermelon." The "watermelon" was a carved, Styrofoam fixture that separated the buffet line from the tables in the eating area. If one looked at it real close, you could see the food stains and nicks that covered the front.

"10-4."

Millie turned to go. "You need to take the dress to Detective Patterson. It's evidence."

Chloe followed her to the door. "So maybe we can work together to track down my sister's killer?"

Chloe kept saying her "sister's killer" but there was no mention of poor Kyle.

Millie's eyes wandered to Chloe's long-sleeved blouse, which was odd considering they were in the tropics.

Chloe followed Millie into the hall. The poor thing looked so sad! Millie impulsively turned around and hugged her slender shoulders, which trembled ever so slightly. "I'll see what I can do," she promised.

"Thank you," Chloe replied thickly. She pressed a hand to her forehead. "I think I need to go lie down."

Chapter 9

Millie jogged down the corridor to the staircase. She took the stairs two at a time. She forgot how many floors it was from Deck 4 to the lido deck, which was where *Waves*, the ship's buffet area, was located.

Andy was already waiting for Millie when she reached the watermelon. He narrowed his eyes when she got close. "What happened to you?"

"I-I. Well, I ran in Chloe Earhart, Courtney's twin sister, down near guest services. She's beside herself what with her sister's death."

Andy crossed his arms and rocked back on his heels. "Why on earth didn't she get off the ship with her sister?"

"She's convinced her sister was murdered and seems determined to get to the bottom of it."

Andy tapped the side of his face. "Ah, I see. So you offered to help find her sister's killer?"

Millie shrugged. "Kind of...sort of."

He waved his hand. "You know, since you were the last person to see Courtney alive, Dave Patterson will want to speak to you."

That didn't bother Millie. What did bother her was the fact she was getting a reputation for being a busy body, which she didn't think she was. It wasn't her fault she just happened to be in the wrong place at the wrong time.

She thought about Dave. He was a nice enough guy. She wasn't sure that he liked her. After all, she always seemed to be underfoot and in his way.

"You still have your list for today?" The "list" was Millie's list of duties. She patted her top pocket. "Right here. In an hour, I report to stage to help Alison with the line dancing class." Alison was one of the other dancers. Millie liked her but didn't really know her all that well. Actually, the only one she really knew was Zack.

She decided she needed to get to know them all a bit better. One never knew when they might come in handy while investigating a murder!

"C'mon." Andy waved his arm. "Let's eat."

Millie followed Andy over to the pizza counter. She eyed the pies in the display case. "What do you recommend?"

"Hawaiian is my favorite but the pepperoni is pretty good, too."

Millie grabbed a slice of pepperoni pizza along with a small side dish of pasta salad. The two wandered to a table in the corner. "Oh! I almost forgot. The captain would like to see you up on the bridge at 1400 hours. To you civilians, that would be 2:00 this afternoon."

Millie had just taken a bite of her pepperoni pizza. It tasted delicious, at least the first bite. Now it felt like she was chewing on a chunk of cardboard. She chewed a few more bites and then swallowed the thick lump.

Millie grabbed her glass of water and took a big swig to wash it down. "W-why me?"

He shrugged. "Maybe he wants to talk to you about the murder."

"You think he suspects me?"

Andy wasn't quite sure, and he wasn't one to question the captain. It was as much a mystery to Andy as it was to Millie.

"I don't know, Millie," he admitted. "All I can tell you is in all my years as cruise director, Captain Armati has never asked to see my assistant."

If that was supposed to make Millie feel better, it didn't. In fact, it had the opposite effect. Her brow began to sweat at the thought of Captain Armati. She'd met him only once. On her very first day and she got the distinct impression he didn't care for her.

Maybe he was going to fire her! "Do you think I'm getting the boot?"

Andy picked a chunk of pineapple from the top of his slice of pizza and popped it into his mouth. "Well, I would hope he would have given me some sort of warning if that was his intent."

Andy picked up his glass of lemonade and took a long swallow. "Of course, he may not tell me in case I tip you off."

That made sense to Millie. Certain she was about to get the ax only days into her new job, she shoved the plate and the rest of her pizza aside. She had completely lost her appetite. *What would she tell her children? That their mother, the loser, had managed to be fired less than a month into the first paid job she'd had in years?*

Andy reached over and patted her hand. "Don't worry about it. If that's the case, I'll try to go to bat for you."

"If I have to get another assistant, that means I'll have to share my cabin again." He winked.

Andy had it made. His cabin was a bit larger than the rest of the staff. It was large enough to accommodate a small table and a couple chairs. There was also a sofa and nice, new flat screen TV.

Plus, Millie couldn't guarantee, but his bath sure seemed a bit bigger than the one she and Sarah shared, which was barely big enough to turn around. Every time Millie climbed into the shower and turned even just a little, the shower curtain clung to her!

"Well, that makes me feel better," she said grimly.

Andy placed his empty plates on his tray and stood. "Let me know as soon as the meeting is over. I'm opening for the afternoon galley tour and will be back in my office after that."

Andy didn't really have an "office." It was more of a cubby tucked back in the corner, behind the dressing room at the back of the stage.

Millie's steps dragged as she made her way to the theater for the line dancing, as if she was making her way to her own execution. She wondered how she'd gotten herself into this predicament. She was beginning to take a real shine to the job, getting to know some of the crew and staff. Millie was making friends, solving murders, and they were paying her for it! Finally, she had purpose in her life again.

The thought of going back to the suburbs and facing the four walls, wandering around with nothing to do and sinking back into a depression was not what she wanted to do. Maybe she could beg him for mercy. Surely the man had some sort of compassion. She could explain her situation.

Her steps lightened. That was what she was going to do! Plead her case. There was no way Captain Armati could fire her if she told him how much the job meant to her!

Millie picked up the pace as she entered the theater. When she spotted Alison setting up on stage, Millie rolled up her sleeves and bound up the steps. "Let's get this show on the road!"

Chapter 10

The line dancing class was way more fun than Millie had thought it would be. Along with Alison, there was another young dancer, Tara. Millie took an immediate liking to Tara. She was bubbly and she smiled all the time. Whenever she looked at Millie, her eyes twinkled with mischief. As if she was about to get in trouble but because she was so sweet, it wouldn't matter.

She and Alison seemed to like each other and the two women taught not only the 15 or so passengers some basic line dance steps, they taught Millie, who had never kicked up a pair of cowboy boots in her life.

It took her a little bit to get the hang of it and she was glad no one she knew was there to watch her embarrass herself, but the girls were patient and they made it fun. The passengers were having a ball and soon, they were groovin' to Achy Breaky Heart.

When the class was over, Millie's feet were sore, but her face was smiling. She thanked both of the girls for showing her the steps. Millie guessed she had done an okay job with her new task because they asked her if she wanted to come back and help the next afternoon when they taught a square dance class.

Millie was thrilled. Square dancing was right up her alley. She nodded. "I can cut the rug with the best of 'em."

Tara's eyes twinkled. "Well, maybe you can show us a thing or two."

Millie was still smiling – sweating – but still smiling – as she walked off the stage and made her way out of the theater. The smile lasted right up until the moment she remembered she was to meet Captain Armati. She glanced down at her watch. She had ten minutes to make it up to the bridge.

Millie's steps dragged as she made her way to the bridge. The captain held her very future in his hands. With just a single word, her world could come crashing down around her!

Millie's hand shook as she tapped on the outer door that opened to the bridge. She sucked in her breath, closed her eyes and whispered a small prayer. "Please God. Let me keep this job. You know how much it means to me."

The door swung open. Millie flashed startled eyes at the man in the doorway. His outfit was similar to Captain Armati's uniform, complete with the stars and bars on the shoulders.

She glanced down at the tag. *Staff Captain Antonio Vitale.* His brown eyes were warm and welcoming. A small smile played across his lips as he looked at Millie's tag. "Ahh. The infamous Mildred Sanders."

His heavy accent was charming and if Millie weren't so dang nervous, it would sound downright sexy. But she was nervous. So nervous that her armpits were damp and her mouth dry. She wished it were the other way around. Her mouth moist and her armpits dry.

She sucked in a breath and smiled brightly. She held out her hand. "How do you do. Uh, Captain Vital."

Millie just about passed out. It wasn't Captain Vital. It was Captain Vitale! The man chuckled. "Vital, Vitale. It's all the same." He waved a hand to the side. "Please. Please come in. Captain Armati is expecting you."

Millie groaned inwardly. That's what terrified her. Expectations. Expectations she was certain she was not living up to. *Why, oh why, could she not behave herself? Why did she have to prove that she could be just as good a detective as her ex-husband, Roger, had been?*

Captain Vitale cocked his head. "Follow me, please."

Millie obediently trudged behind the captain as he walked down the narrow hall and into the bridge. There were only two other people inside: a woman in uniform and Captain Armati. The woman was off to one side, studying what looked like an oversized computer screen.

Captain Armati was front and center. He held a pair of binoculars to his eyes as he studied the vast ocean through the wall of windows.

Millie wished she hadn't been so nervous. It would be cool to stand there and check out the view. All that water. The amazing thing was - the captain knew exactly where they were at – and where they were going.

Millie wished she felt the same. She had no idea where she was going. Probably home.

Captain Armati set the binoculars on the top of the counter. He shifted his body, his gaze coming to rest on Millie. The sweat had traveled from her armpits to the top of her forehead as beads of perspiration formed on her brow. Millie was so freaked out, she didn't even wipe it away. Soon it would be trickling into her eyes. No matter. She would be history and this whole moment of sheer terror forgotten.

The captain skipped the pleasantries. "Millie Sanders. Follow me." He didn't wait for an answer. Instead, he abruptly headed to the other side of the bridge - the opposite end from where Millie had just come in. She picked up the pace and trailed along as he walked down a small corridor. At the end of the small hall was a gray metal door marked "Private." Above the silver door lever was a key pad.

Captain Armati punched in a code and opened the door. He stepped inside and held the door. "Please. Come in."

Millie let out the breath she'd been holding. He had said "please." Maybe she wasn't in as deep of doo-doo as she originally imagined.

There was no time to dwell on the *please* part. Millie looked around. She was in some sort of private apartment. Her eyes widened as it dawned on her that this had to be Captain Armati's private quarters!

It was a masculine space. A dark, gray sofa sat against the far wall. In front of that was a round wooden coffee table. On the other side of the room was a flat screen TV that hung on the wall.

Next to the TV were two floor-to-ceiling bookcases, crammed full of books. A wingback chair was directly in front of the bookcases and a tall lamp with an ornate, Victorian shade hovered over the top of the wingback.

It was the perfect spot to read a book, escape the hordes of passengers or avoid complaining crew.

It was definitely a cozy retreat.

Beyond the living room was a small kitchenette. Millie couldn't see the whole thing. Only enough to know there was a small stove, a sink and enough counter space to cook a gourmet meal.

Millie didn't want to seem as if she was snooping. She lowered her eyes and studied her fingernails. Her palms were sweating. She rubbed them on the front of her pants.

Captain Armati stepped past the living room and stopped in front of the floor-to-ceiling windows on the other side of the room. Millie, unsure what she should do, followed him. Plus, she wanted to check out the view. This was a whole lot different from her little hole in the wall. Windowless, claustrophobic hole in the wall. Still, she was grateful for her job.

Which was in jeopardy. The fear came rushing back as she followed the captain's gaze and stared out the window, certain this was one of the last times she would have a view such as this. There were absolutely zero views like this in the suburbs of Grand Rapids!

Captain Armati put his hands behind his back. He nodded out the window. "I love the ocean."

Millie nodded. "Me, too."

He glanced at Millie. "It's in my blood. You know, my father was a captain."

She didn't know that but Millie nodded anyways.

He went on. "Spent his whole life sailing the world." He abruptly changed the subject. "Do you like working on the ship?"

"I-uh. Yes, sir. I mean, yes, Captain Armati." The words stuck in her mouth like six saltine crackers without a drop of water to wash them down. "I love the job," she admitted. There. It was out. He could fire her, but at least he would know he was destroying her dreams!

He held up a hand. "Stay here."

He didn't wait for an answer. He deftly sidestepped Millie and headed up the stairs on the opposite side of the room. Stairs Millie hadn't even noticed.

Her eyes followed him up. The wonder of it all! This place had a second floor!

117

She watched him stroll across the open loft and disappear behind a door. If he was going to fire her, he was being nice about it. Maybe this was some sort of test. Then she remembered Andy saying that the captain had never asked an assistant cruise director to come to the bridge.

Millie nervously shifted from foot to foot. He was taking forever! The minutes dragged by. Maybe something happened to him. Like he suddenly became ill. She wondered if she should go check on him.

Millie took a step in the direction when the upper door suddenly opened. The captain was back – and he wasn't alone. There, trotting along beside him was one of the cutest little dogs Millie had ever seen. He wasn't much bigger than a doggie dish.

"Yip!" The little ball of fur eyed Millie before he scooted down the stairs and darted to her. He raced around her feet a few times before stepping on her shoes and lifting his front legs. He pawed at her shins.

The captain looked down at the bundle of fur sitting on Millie's feet. "This is Scout."

Millie bent over and stuck her hand out so Scout could sniff it. Then she reached out to rub the tip of Scout's ear.

Captain Armati sighed. "The dog is a gift from my daughter, Fiona."

Scout ran over to the captain who promptly picked him up. The dog nuzzled his neck. Millie did a mental shake. This man loved that little dog. But the ship didn't allow dogs - or any animals for that matter. That was, of course, unless you were the captain.

"Scout is a birthday present," he explained.

He set the wisp of a dog down. The dog ran back to Millie and pawed at her ankle. She picked him up and held him close. Close enough for him to lick the end of her nose. The dog was adorable.

Scout was a cute name. She remembered her dog, Daisy. Sudden tears welled in the back of her eyes. Millie blinked rapidly.

She hoped the Captain hadn't noticed, but he had. "You don't like dogs?"

Millie sucked in a breath. "I love dogs. My dog, Daisy, died a few months back. Daisy's death was the last straw. She was the reason I decided to apply for a job on the ship. Once she was gone, nobody back home needed me."

Captain Armati stepped close to Millie. "I'm sorry."

Millie nodded. "Me, too."

Scout was trying to climb the front of Millie. He got hold of a chunk of her hair that had come loose from the tidy bun and began to gnaw on it. The crazy thing was cuter than a button. How could anyone not become attached?

"I was hoping you could help me out," he said.

Millie set Scout on the floor. He ran over to a small box of stuffed animals in the corner of the room and proceeded to drag a stuffed monkey — twice as big as he was — across the floor. He stopped in front of Millie and looked up. "Ruff!"

"Scout gets lonely in here all day. I need someone who can take him around. You know, keep him company. I thought of you."

Millie nodded. Perhaps it was because she was the most "grandmotherly" of the staff and crew.

Captain Armati studied her face. "Of course, only if you're interested."

Was she ever interested! Millie interrupted. "Oh, I would love to help out! Take Scout for walks, take him around the ship." She paused. "Can I take him with me around the ship?"

Scout could be her sidekick, her partner in crime...her miniature sleuth!

Captain Armati nodded. "Of course. I have permission to keep the dog on board with me. I guess you could say corporate bent a rule or two on my behalf. As long as Scout doesn't become a nuisance," he warned.

That meant Millie would be responsible for making sure the dog didn't get in trouble. Heck! Millie couldn't even keep herself out of trouble!

"Are you sure?"

Millie nodded.

The captain grinned. "You have a bit of a reputation as a busybody, but I think you're the perfect person for this job, if you're up to it."

"I'll leave a small baggie of food in the table," he continued. "Scout eats a little bit all day."

Scout knew they were talking about him! He barked and then danced around in little circles. It was if he somehow knew his life was about to get a lot more exciting.

Captain Armati picked Scout up and headed for the balcony. "Let me show you around."

He unlatched the hook and slid the slider open. The three of them stepped outside. Millie could almost be envious of the balcony. It was large. On one end were two lounge chairs, a small glass top table next to each. On the other side was a long, green strip of AstroTurf...a spot that apparently belonged to Scout.

The captain set the pup down. Scout pranced over to the strip and routed around, pawing at the fake grass, before darting to the other end to take care of business.

After Scout was done, they walked back inside the cabin. The captain quietly closed the door and locked it. "I was thinking you could come up in the morning before your shift started, take Scout out and then go back on duty until lunchtime. After that maybe run back up here in the evening for another go 'round the ship. Kind of wear him out so he'll sleep at night."

That would be fine with Millie. In fact, that would be more than fine! She loved the idea! On top of that, it meant that Millie wasn't about to be fired. It felt more like a promotion!

Captain Armati walked Millie to the apartment door. He put his hand on the door handle and paused. "Or, if you want, you can pick him up later today...maybe later this afternoon?"

Millie reached down and patted the furry brown head. Scout licked her hand and wagged his little stub of a tail. "Sure! Why not? I'll be back at 4:00!"

Captain Armati opened the door. "I heard you're snooping around, asking questions about the man overboard and his fiancé that committed suicide."

Millie's heart sank. She knew it was too good to be true. The other shoe had finally dropped. She sucked in a breath and waited for the reprimand she knew was forthcoming.

"Try to stay out of trouble this time," he warned. "You have enough to keep yourself busy without trying to solve already-solved crimes."

Millie opened an eye and peeked at him. The captain was smiling. He picked up his tiny pooch. "Scout's a good watch dog. He'll yip at anything." Scout wriggled around and licked the captain's chin, which made them both laugh.

"His case is here if you want to take it with you." There, lying on the floor next to the door, was what looked like a small overnight bag. Millie picked it up. It reminded her of a Louis Vuitton bag. Except one end unzipped halfway. It would be perfect for carrying Scout around the ship!

Millie patted Scout's head. "See you later Scout."

"Yip!"

Millie stepped outside and the captain closed the door behind her. Her steps were light. Millie almost floated across the bridge.

Staff Captain Vitale grinned at her. "Looks like you got a new duty to add to the list."

"More like a promotion," Millie joked.

Chapter 11

Andy was waiting for her inside his small cubby when she wandered to the back of the theater. "Well? What happened?"

Millie stared at him stone-faced. "I got a promotion. Captain gave me your job."

Andy's face turned pale. His mouth dropped open. "You're kidding."

Millie grinned mischievously. "Yes, of course I am. No one can take your place!"

Andy dropped the pen he'd been holding. He slammed the palm of his hand on the Formica tabletop. "You're gonna give an old man a heart attack!"

"You're younger than me," Millie pointed out.

"True," Andy admitted. "So what did happen?"

"I have a new sidekick. Scout."

"Scout?" Andy was confused. He knew the name of every single crew and staff on the ship. There was no one by the name of "Scout."

"It's Captain Armati's dog. A Teacup Yorkie to be precise."

For the second time, Andy's mouth fell open. "There's a dog on the ship?" He had heard rumors – hints of a dog on board - but he'd never seen an animal. To him, it was always nothing more than a bunch of gossip.

Millie nodded. "He's about this big." She held out her hands.

Andy leaned back in the chair. He crossed his arms. "So you're saying Captain Armati has a dog, the dog is on this ship and he put you in charge of this Scout?"

"Yep. Starting later today. I pick Scout up at 4:00 to make our first rounds together."

Andy Walker had heard it all. His eyes narrowed as he studied Millie. This woman had been on the ship just a short amount of time. So far, there had been a murder, a man overboard, a suicide and now there was a dog on the ship? It was almost as if no matter where Millie went, something crazy happened.

He couldn't really call it a "black cloud" following her around. More like a microburst of cosmic energy that surrounded her. In all his years working with Captain Armati, he couldn't remember the captain confiding in any of the staff. For him to single Millie out to take care of his pet was a bit unbelievable.

He leaned forward. "How do you do it?"

"Do what?"

"I dunno. Get people to..." He waved his hand in the air. "Take for example, Cat. She doesn't like anyone on board the ship and now you two are best buds."

"We weren't in the beginning," Millie pointed out. "Yeah, I guess she does like me. Maybe I'm not a threat. You know, more like a grandmotherly-type."

"Hmm." Andy leaned back in his chair. Maybe Millie was right. She wasn't threatening. She did have that grandmother look about her. In addition to that, she was nice, even if she was a bit on the nosy side.

Andy remembered Millie mentioning her ex-husband. How lonely she had been after he left her. It was one of the reasons she'd applied for the assistant cruise director job in the first place.

Well, as long as Millie wasn't after his job, she could watch the do and walk the dog. He changed the subject. "How's the investigation going?"

Millie mentioned the friends that were in the cabin on the other side of Courtney and Kyle's.

"Let me guess. "You're going to talk to them."

Millie nodded. "After I pick up Scout."

Andy stood.

"You want me to bring Scout by?" she asked.

Andy nodded. "Sure. I can't wait to see a broken company policy live and in action," he said wryly.

Millie's brows furrowed. "Captain Armati said he had permission."

Millie would feel terrible if she got Captain Armati in trouble. She was having second thoughts about taking the dog out in public, but the captain was the one that told her to do just that.

The rest of the afternoon dragged by. Millie was anxious to start her dog sitting duties. She hadn't realized how much she missed Daisy. Hopefully, Scout and she wouldn't become too attached to each other. If something happened and Scout had to leave the ship, she would feel terrible.

Millie shoved her fears aside and wandered back to the cabin. Sarah was inside, getting ready for her shift. She brushed her hair as she glanced at Millie in the mirror. "Did you know there were two more deaths on board the ship?"

"Yeah. Hard to believe." Millie unclipped the two-way radio from her hip and set it on top of her bed. "Such a sad situation. They're calling it murder/suicide."

Sarah tilted her head and ran her fingers through her straight, dark hair. "What do you think?"

"I'm not sure about the young man's death but I don't think the young woman committed suicide."

Sarah set the brush down and stared at her reflection. "Why do you think that?"

Millie sighed as she sank down on the edge of the bed. "Because I was the last one to see that poor girl and she was in no condition to commit suicide. She had passed out on the bed."

Sarah straightened her nametag. "Are you a suspect?"

Millie was certain that even if she wasn't a suspect, Dave Patterson would be tracking her down soon to ask her what she knew.

After Sarah left, Millie slipped off her shoes and lay down on the bed. She stared up at the bottom of Sarah's bunk. The last 24 hours had been harrowing. She was beginning to wonder if she was coming or going.

The good news was, she wasn't being fired. The bad news was, the more she learned about Kyle and Courtney, the more suspects that kept popping up: Chloe, the twin sister. Zack, the ex-boyfriend. Courtney herself, even though she was no longer around to defend herself, God rest her soul.

Millie's eyes narrowed. But what about the couple's friends? Adam and Melissa. Millie was a good judge of character. She would be able to tell right off the bat if the two of them were hiding something.

Chapter 12

Millie's eyes flew open. She must have dozed off. She glanced down at her watch. It was almost four. Almost time to start her doggie duties and she didn't want to be late!

She slipped her feet into her shoes and stepped over to the mirror. Her hair stuck out in all different directions. Millie quickly pulled her hair into a ponytail, twisted it in a tight bun and stuck a hair clip over the top. She grabbed her radio and raced out the door.

Millie made it to the bridge with a minute and a half to spare! Captain Armati was standing in the middle of the bridge, in front of the large panel of gadgets. He turned when he saw her. "Scout's ready to go."

He walked Millie down the small hall to the door that separated the bridge and his apartment. He pressed the buttons on the keypad and pushed the door open. Scout was waiting on the other side.

Millie covered her mouth to stifle her laugh. Scout, decked out in a miniature sailor suit and round white sailor cap, wagged his tail when he saw Millie. He trotted over and climbed up on her foot. "Woof!"

She picked him up and held him close. "Look at Mr. Spiffy, all ready to see the sights."

Captain Armati patted the top of his head. "I think he knows. Somehow the crazy dog knows."

Millie grabbed Scout's bag and the two stepped into the bridge. "What time should I have him back?"

"Your shift ends at..."

"10:30," Millie told him.

"Right. Just bring Scout back after you've finished your shift."

He gently tugged Scout's ear. "Behave," he warned him.

Scout was a bit of a wiggle worm as they walked. He knew he was going somewhere. Somewhere he'd never been.

Millie shifted the bag on her shoulder and pulled Scout close. It was time to set the ground rules. "You need to stay with me. This is a big ship and I don't need you getting lost," she told him.

"Yip!"

Happy hour trivia wasn't scheduled to start for another hour. Millie's stomach growled. She remembered how she hadn't finished her pizza, thinking that she was about to be canned. "Let's go grab a bite to eat."

Millie took the outside deck as she headed toward the buffet. It would give Scout a chance to enjoy some fresh air. Millie clipped the leash to his collar and set him on the ground. The doggie leash was almost as big as he was.

Scout's little tongue hung out of his mouth as he trotted next to Millie. His brown eyes darted back and forth, as he tried to take everything in.

He got a few looks from passengers, which quickly turned to smiles as they bent down to pet him. Scout was eating it up!

When they got outside the restaurant, she opened the bag and set him inside. She left the top half open so he could peek out. She hadn't asked the captain if Scout could have snacks.

She thought about Daisy, her beloved dog that had died. Surely a tiny piece of chicken or beef couldn't hurt. As she moved along the buffet, she could see Scout's round little nose move up and down as he sniffed the air.

Millie filled a plate and she and Scout headed back outside to one of the bistro tables. She set Scout and the bag on top of the table.

The first thing she did was slice a chunk of prime rib into tiny pieces. She held it out for Scout who promptly licked her hand, then devoured the small pieces of meat. He ate it so fast, Millie thought the poor fellow was starving. She carved a second piece. Scout devoured that piece just as fast!

Millie stopped at three pieces. The last thing she needed to do was make the poor thing sick! He continued to watch her with that same hungry look so she turned the bag out. The sights and sounds around him easily distracted Scout. He no longer cared about food.

His head popped all the way out of the bag. His ears moved back and forth like two furry rotating radars as he watched passengers pass by.

Millie finished her meal and began placing the empty dishes back on the tray. She took a sip of water and set the glass next to the plate.

A young couple stopped near the table. With them was a young girl who couldn't have been more than 4 or 5 years old. She pointed at Scout. "Dog."

"There's no dog," the woman said. She grasped the little girl's hand and urged her on.

The girl stubbornly refused to move. "There." She pointed again.

The man followed the child's finger. He bent down. "Well, you're right Maisie. That is a dog."

He held out his hand. "Hi there, fella."

Scout licked the tip of his finger and barked.

The girl – Maisie – reached her hand into the carrier to pet Scout. "Pretty," she said. Scout's whole body shifted inside his carrier as he tried to get close to the little girl.

The man and woman exchanged glances over the top of the girl's head.

Millie set her tray and leftovers on the chair beside her. She unzipped the rest of Scout's bag and lifted him out. She held him in her lap. "Would you like to pet him?"

Maisie tentatively ran a small hand down Scout's back.

"His name is Scout," Millie told the little girl.

"Scout." The little girl repeated the name.

The woman turned her head away, tears rolling down her cheeks.

Millie's eyes shot up. Something was going on here. Dogs don't normally make people cry. Not unless it was a beloved pet who had just died. It made her think of Daisy.

Millie and Scout stood. "Would you like to hold Scout?" she asked Maisie.

"Yes please." The little girl promptly settled into the seat next to Millie and held out her hands. Millie gently set Scout in the girl's lap.

He wiggled, wriggled, and licked the little girl, which made her giggle.

The man kneeled on the deck. Millie watched as a single tear trickled down his cheek. He pet Scout's head. "Would you like a dog?" the man asked the little girl.

She nodded but never took her eyes from Scout. Finally, the man gently took Scout from the little girl's lap and handed him to Millie.

"Let's go get some ice cream." He took the little girl's hand and led her inside. The woman hung behind. She watched as Millie put Scout back in the case.

"My little girl. Those are the first words she's spoken in over a month," she explained.

Millie gazed through the sliding glass doors. She watched as the man filled a cone with ice cream and handed it to his daughter.

The woman went on. "Our house caught fire and burned to the ground. We almost lost Maisie in the blaze."

The woman's blue eyes stared into Millie's eyes. "Thank you."

The man and Maisie were back now. Millie bent down. "Would you like to see Scout again?"

The girl licked her chocolate cone, her somber eyes sparked. "Yes!"

Millie nodded. "Scout and I will be back here tomorrow at the same time," she promised.

The girl reached for her mother's hand. She looked up, her blue eyes pleading. "Can we see Scout again?"

"Absolutely." She hugged the girl close. As the couple walked off the man mouthed the words, "Thank you!"

Millie and Scout watched them until they disappeared from sight. She patted Scout's head. "Well, look at you...already making friends!"

She lifted Scout with one hand and his bag with the other. The two of them wandered across the deck. It was time for trivia.

Millie set Scout on top of the piano and unlocked the cabinet. They had arrived a few minutes early, which was good. It gave Millie time to organize trivia and make sure Scout was ready to meet more guests.

As the guests came forward to pick up their pencils and pads of paper, Scout got more oohs and aahs than 4th of July fireworks. He was the hit of the trivia time. Even after the game was over, most of the guests stopped back by to tell him good-bye. Several asked if he would be back again.

Millie headed to Cat's gift shop. Cat spied Scout right away. "I heard you had a dog." She reached over and lifted Scout from the case. "Look at the adorable sailor suit," she cooed. She pulled him close. "He's precious. Is it true he belongs to the captain?"

Millie nodded as Cat set Scout on the floor. She didn't let him get too far. Just in the back near where they were standing. There were guests inside the store shopping and Millie was concerned someone might not see him and step on him by accident.

With one eye on Scout, Millie turned to Cat. "Time for a meeting to go over what we have," she said. "Can you meet later tonight?"

Cat smoothed back her hair. "Yes. I have some new info, too. I had a chance to talk to the other couple. I think their names are Aaron and..."

"You mean Adam and Melissa?"

She snapped her fingers. "Yep. Those are the ones. You'll never believe what they told me about Courtney's twin sister, Chloe."

Great! Millie planned to invite Chloe along for the meeting. But if they were going to be talking about her, that wouldn't work! She shelved the idea. For now. Maybe next time. "I better track down Annette." She lifted Scout up and set him back in his carrier. "How does 11:00 sound?" It would give her time to finish her shift and drop Scout off.

"Let's not do the library this time. Too many people in the vicinity if you know what I mean," Cat said.

Millie nodded. She was probably right. They needed to stay under the radar. "What about the kitchen?"

The last time Annette and Millie had met in the kitchen, they not only came up with great

ideas for solving poor Olivia's murder, they
baked up a storm!

Millie left the store and headed to the kitchen
to find Annette, which was easy to do. She heard
Annette before she saw her. She was scolding
someone. Rather loudly. Which wasn't like
Annette. She was normally calm, cool and
collected. But not at that moment. She was
letting someone have it!

"If I ever catch you cutting corners like that
again, I'll toss you overboard myself," she
threatened.

The tone of Annette's voice made Millie
squirm and Scout's ears go flat. He let out a
whimper. Millie patted his head. "Don't worry.
Her bark is worse than her bite," she reassured
him.

They rounded the corner and found Annette,
rolling pin in her hand. Holding it more like a
weapon, Millie decided. She started to back away
but Annette spied her. It was too late. The scowl

changed to a smile. She waved Millie in. "You're just in time to see me commit a murder."

Annette's gaze settled on a young man who was on the other side of the counter. "Amit, here, decided that we didn't need to use real butter for the lobster dipping sauce. He singlehandedly decided that margarine would work just fine!"

Annette's face began to redden at the thought. "Can you believe that? Margarine! Might as well have just used Milk of Magnesia." She scowled.

Amit cowered. Millie felt sorry for the poor fellow. She made a mental note to never, ever substitute anything in Annette's kitchen!

Her look softened when she spotted the perky little face peeking out of the bag hanging from Millie's shoulder. "I heard you had a dog." Annette reached down and rubbed Scout's ears. "Hey there fella. Why, aren't you as adorable as all get out?"

She looked up at Millie. "You really are trying to get fired, sneaking a dog on board." She thrust a hand on her hip.

Millie grinned. "I doubt I'll get fired. Scout belongs to Captain Armati."

Annette's eyebrow shot up. "You don't say!"

Millie set the bag on the floor and unzipped the front. Scout gingerly placed one paw on the cold tile floor. He looked to the left, then the right before he stuck his nose in the air and trotted over to the edge of the counter. The kitchen was a slice of doggie heaven!

It took a few minutes for Scout to become brave enough to venture around but when he did, he took off like a rocket ship. He wandered here and there. Unfortunately, for poor Scout, the kitchen floor was spotless. There wasn't a scrap of food for him to nibble on.

"Can we meet here at 11:00?" Millie looked from Scout to Annette.

"Of course. What's on the menu?"

Millie was craving banana bread. Something she hadn't had in months. Long before she ever boarded the cruise ship. "What about banana bread?"

Annette nodded. "Perfect. Some of the bananas are getting too ripe. We can make some loaves tonight and the staff can put them out for breakfast in the morning."

Scout was back. He plopped down at Millie's feet, waiting for her to pick him up. "I have some info on the you-know-what." She leaned in. "Room service delivered to one Courtney Earhart's room the night of her death."

Millie's eyes widened. "What time?"

"One in the morning."

One in the morning...not long after Millie had left the unconscious girl in bed. She couldn't wait to hear that one. Plus, Cat had some info now, too. This investigation was starting to shape up!

Chapter 13

Scout was as good as gold the entire time Millie had him with her.

She gave Captain Armati a glowing report. She told him how the passengers adored Scout. She even mentioned the little girl, Maisie, that hadn't talked in weeks and how she promised to meet the family in the same spot the next day so she could visit with Scout again.

Captain Armati thanked Millie for taking Scout out. She told him she'd be back in the morning to pick him up.

Millie nuzzled Scout's head. "See you in the morning." Scout's sad brown eyes followed Millie to the door. He whined when she opened it.

Millie smiled at Staff Captain Vitale on her way out.

It was still a little too early to head to the kitchen. The crew would be cleaning up after the dinner crowd. The headliner show would be starting in a few minutes so Millie headed to the theater.

She stood in the back and watched the magician perform some of his tricks. Millie always wondered how they did some of the stuff they did. Years of practice, she decided.

The show finally ended. Millie stood off to the side and watched as the passengers exited the theater. More like stampeded. She waited for the theater to finish clearing out and was almost ready to head to the kitchen when she caught a glimpse of two vaguely familiar figures. It was Adam and Melissa West: Courtney and Kyle's friends. They weren't alone. They were talking to another couple as they walked.

Millie faded into the shadow of the door. She didn't want them to spot her. Her eyes narrowed. The other couple they were with was even more interesting than the Wests themselves. The other couple was the couple

Millie had met earlier. Maisie's parents. The ones with the little girl who wouldn't talk!

Millie could see they weren't having a casual conversation amongst strangers. No, the four of them knew each other. Millie's suspicions were confirmed when Melissa West picked Maisie up and hugged her tight. That meant that Kyle and Courtney had not only traveled on board with Courtney's sister, Chloe, and the Wests, this other couple somehow knew them.

Millie stood there for several long moments. Why hadn't Chloe mentioned the other couple? She had told her about the Wests.

She headed upstairs to the kitchen. Surely, somewhere there was video footage of passengers boarding the ship, not to mention the manifest – a way to track passengers that were sailing together.

Annette and Cat were already in the kitchen when Millie got there. Spread out across the expansive counter were all of the ingredients for banana nut bread. Cat was mashing bananas in a bowl while Annette mixed the dry ingredients. She handed Millie a stack of bread tins. "Here. Grease these." She stuck a stick of butter in Millie's hands.

Millie pulled an apron over her head. She tied the back and grabbed the tin on top of the stack.

Cat peeled a ripe banana and dropped it in the bowl in front of her. "Melissa and Adam West are getting off the ship in Grand Cayman."

The stop in Grand Cayman was a couple days away. South Seas Cay, the ship's private island, was their next stop.

"What about the other couple with them? Are they getting off, too?"

Annette dropped her fork on the counter. "What other couple?"

"The couple I saw exiting the theater with the Wests just a few minutes ago."

Annette picked the fork back up and began sifting the ingredients. She paused long enough to drop a teaspoon of salt into the mix. "So how many suspects do we have now?"

Millie reached for another tin. She lifted an index finger. "Chloe." She raised a second finger. "The Wests, the mystery couple." She put her hand back down. "And don't forget Courtney herself." Not that Millie believed that for a minute. Something smelled fishy and it wasn't the ocean!

Annette cracked an egg in a second bowl. "Now what?"

Millie finished greasing the pans. She slid them over to Annette. "We need to take a peek at the manifest. You know, find out who boarded with whom."

Cat wrinkled her nose. "I'm sure Dave Patterson has already done that."

Millie frowned. True. He probably had.
Maybe she should visit him in the morning.
Honestly, she was surprised he hadn't tracked
her down and interrogated her. Of course, with
the list of suspects growing, he probably hadn't
made it that far down the list.

The girls finished mixing the bread and
Annette popped the pans into the oven.

Annette turned to the cabinet behind her, bent
down and opened the door. She pulled out a tray
of tempting treats and set them on the counter.

Millie leaned in. Her mouth began to water.
"What are those?"

"Coconut key lime bites," Annette told her.
"Here...try one." She lifted the plastic cover and
pulled two out. She handed one to Cat and the
other to Millie.

Millie nibbled the corner. It was tart, coconut,
sweet, and it melted in Millie's mouth. She rolled

her eyes. "These are heavenly. You should call them 'A Taste of Heaven Coconut Bites.'"

Cat bit into hers. The tart lime made her mouth pucker. Then the sweet took over and rolled over her tongue like a layer of sugarcoated coconut.

Annette plucked one out and popped it in her mouth. "You like them? These are just an experiment. No recipe or anything."

Millie reached for another one. "I hope you remember how to make them. I need this recipe." Not that Millie had anywhere to make them, but she could save it for someday when she went back home.

Annette handed one more to Cat and then tucked the plastic covering over the goodies. She slid the tray back into the cabinet and closed the door. "That's my private stash."

When the bread had finished baking, Annette pulled the dozen loaves from the oven and left them on the counter nearby to cool. She sliced one of the loaves into thirds and wrapped them in tinfoil. She handed one to Cat and the other to Millie.

Millie's eyes burned as she looked down at the banana bread. It reminded her of home. She blinked back the tears. *Why would something so small, so simple affect her like that? She must be exhausted*, she decided.

Annette waited until Cat and Millie were out of the kitchen before she turned off the light. Millie glanced in the mirror on the wall on her way out of the dining room. She barely recognized her own reflection. She looked tired. Of course, it had been a long couple of days with little sleep.

Tomorrow was a sea day and Millie didn't have to report to Andy's office until after she picked up Scout. She could barely keep her eyes open as she slipped out of her work uniform and into her pajamas.

Millie opened the Bible she kept tucked in the corner of her bed. She flicked on the small light near her head and opened to where she had left off. She smiled as she read Matthew 6:34:

"Therefore do not worry about tomorrow, for tomorrow will worry about its own things. Sufficient for the day is its own trouble."

Millie closed the Bible and shut her eyes. Wasn't that the truth!

Chapter 14

Millie was up early the next morning. Either she had somehow managed to get enough sleep for a change or she was excited to start her day with Scout. Plus, it was a sea day. Unlike tomorrow when she had to be up early and on the first shuttle boat to Majestic Cruise line's private island, South Seas Cay.

Sarah was already gone. Millie had heard her creep out of bed and head to the bathroom hours ago. Sarah had tried to be quiet but their cabin was so small, so compact, you could hear every noise whether your were crawling out of bed or taking a shower.

Millie was getting used to it and had actually fallen back asleep while Sarah was in the bath. Although Sarah was younger than Millie's own daughter, Beth, she was the perfect roommate.

Millie slipped into the shower and wet her hair. She squeezed a glob of shampoo in the palm of her hand and then lathered her hair. Her mind drifted to the events of the day before and her first day with Scout.

She thought about the young couple that had stopped by while Millie was eating her lunch. The ones with the little girl. Her eyes narrowed. What was her name? *Melody? Mandy?* No. Maisie! The little girl's name was Maisie.

They knew Courtney and Kyle. But how?

After Millie dressed, she headed down the I-95 corridor and ran smack dab into Dave Patterson, head of security. "Ah. Just the person I'm looking for."

Millie swallowed hard. It looked like Patterson had finally made his way down the list.

"You have a minute?" He didn't wait for her to reply as he motioned her along. "We can talk in my office." His office wasn't far. It was one deck above the crew quarters but at the other end.

He talked as he walked. "I'm sure you were expecting me."

Millie nodded. "How is your investigation into Kyle Zondervan and Courtney Earhart's untimely deaths going?"

Patterson slipped his key card in the door marked "Security" and pushed it open. He waited for Millie to step inside before following her in. "As you know, it's tentatively being called a murder / suicide."

He nodded to the small metal chair in front of the desk and slipped into the larger, padded chair on the other side. He leaned back in the chair, his fingertips resting on his chin as he studied Millie.

Millie sat nervously on the edge of her seat. Patterson had a way of making her feel as if she were some sort of fascinating bug he was studying under a microscope. Or a nosy woman who couldn't mind her own business, which was probably closer to what he thought, she decided.

"How did you manage to end up in Courtney Earhart's room the night of her death?"

Millie picked an imaginary piece of lint from her sleeve. "I-I uh, ran into her up on deck. She was drunk and didn't seem capable of navigating the steps back to her room so I offered to walk her back to her cabin."

"Then what happened?" he prompted.

"When we finally got to her room," Millie squeezed her hands into small fists, "she-uh. She passed out on her bed. I was worried she was going to choke. You know, she'd thrown up and I figured if she threw up again she might suffocate so I tipped her to the side and propped pillows around her."

Patterson leaned forward. "Then what?"

Millie shook her head. "She was out like a light. That's why I have a hard time believing she was capable of not only writing a suicide note but also swallowing all those pills. She must've thrown up 2 – 3 times before I took her to her cabin."

Patterson nodded thoughtfully. He pulled a manila folder from his top desk drawer and opened the clasp. He pulled out several 5x7 photos. The photos were of Courtney's room, Courtney lying on the bed, and the bottle of pills. He turned the photos around. "Is this what the room looked like when you left?"

Millie slipped her reading glasses on. She studied the first photo. The one of Courtney. "Not quite," she admitted.

"The outfit." Patterson tapped an index finger on top of the photo of Courtney.

Millie finished his sentence. "Was not the outfit Courtney was wearing when I left her cabin. The dress she had been wearing was blue – not pink - and there were stains on the front from her – uh, heaving. And probably spilling a few drinks."

He slid the second photo forward. The one of the bottle of pills. "Do you recall seeing this in her cabin that night? Sitting on the dresser perhaps?"

Millie studied the photo. She closed her eyes, trying to remember that night. "No. I don't recall seeing the pill bottle. Of course, that doesn't mean it wasn't there. It could have been," she admitted.

She opened her eyes to find a set of brilliant blue ones studying her intently. She wriggled in her chair uncomfortably. Dave Patterson had beautiful blue eyes. They were like the ocean and they crinkled kindly.

Millie blushed, hoping he couldn't read her mind. She wasn't convinced that he couldn't. It was as if his eyes were staring into her soul.

He broke the gaze as he reached for the third and final photo. The one of the cabin. "What about the cabin? Is this what it looked like when you left?"

Millie slid her glasses up and grabbed the photo. It was then that she noticed something she hadn't noticed before. "I never realized there was an adjoining door." The door connected Courtney and Kyle's room to the West's room!

"Do you think they're suspects?" Dave Patterson already had the answer to that. He had already talked to Chloe Earhart and knew that Chloe's sister, Courtney, felt as if her life was in danger. Chloe had also alluded to the fact that the Wests had had a falling out with Courtney and Kyle on the flight to Miami.

Millie nodded. "I wouldn't rule anyone out." Which made her remember the other couple. Maisie's parents. "There's another couple with them on the cruise. I'm not sure of their names, though," she admitted.

Patterson gathered the photos and dropped them back inside the envelope. "How do you know?"

"Because I saw them leave the theater last night with the Wests. The way they were acting. They know each other."

Patterson massaged the back of his neck. "Chloe never mentioned another couple."

Millie picked up. "Which is odd. I mean, wouldn't they all be suspects?"

He let go of his neck and began to drum his fingers on the desktop. "I could bring Chloe in for questioning again but maybe we shouldn't tip our hand yet."

"I know how you can find out who they are," Millie told him. "The mysterious couple have a daughter. Her name is Maisie."

Patterson grinned, showing off a brilliant set of pearly-whites. Millie had never seen him smile, or if she had, she was certain she had never seen him smile like that! Her mouth turned into the Sahara Desert in the noonday sun.

"Is there any other tidbit of information you'd like to share?" he prompted.

She slowly shook her head. There was something niggling in the back of her mind but for the life of her, she couldn't figure out what it was. Not when he was smiling at her like that!

He abruptly got to his feet. "Thanks for your help, Millie." He stepped over to the door and opened it. "You'll let me know if you stumble upon anything else?"

Millie nodded. The desert sand was blowing hard. Her tongue was stuck to the roof of her mouth. Millie stepped out of the room and gave a small wave, still not trusting herself to speak.

Dave Patterson watched her for a few seconds and slowly closed the door. He shook his head. Millie Sanders was a bit of an enigma. Like fire

and ice. One minute a chatterbox and the next
she clammed up. He had to wonder how she
ended up right in the thick of things.

Chapter 15

Millie was late. She had five minutes to make it up to the bridge and pick up Scout. She didn't want the captain to think she was irresponsible and shirking her doggie duties. Fortunately, Millie was getting fast at navigating the ship. She was in front of the door to the bridge in four minutes flat with a whole minute to spare.

Captain Armati was off in the corner, talking to Staff Captain Vitale. The two men nodded as Millie made her way across the bridge. Captain Armati met her in the hallway, near the entrance to his private quarters.

He smiled at Millie. "Ready for another day with Scout?" He didn't wait for a reply as he punched in the code that unlocked the door.

Millie caught a whiff of cologne. The smell lingered in the air as she followed behind him. It smelled nice, and expensive, she decided. Her eyes wandered to the back of his gray head. A man in uniform. Captain Armati was an attractive man. She wondered if he was married.

Millie gave a mental shake. What was wrong with her? First, she was getting butterflies in Dave Patterson's office and now she was admiring the back of Captain Armati's head, trying to figure out if he was married!

Was she finally, after all this time, coming back to life again? Millie figured that was all done and over with. That she would never be interested in men again. That she could wrap herself up in so many other projects there wouldn't be room for someone else.

"...and Scout was sound asleep." Captain Armati was talking. Millie wasn't listening. She was still having that internal conversation about joining the living again and showing an interest in the opposite sex.

Millie's mind had wandered and she missed what the captain had said. She blurted out the first thing that popped into her head. "Scout sleeps in your bed?" She had never let Daisy do that. Of course, that was Roger's decision. Millie might have, but Roger had always been adamant there would be no dogs in the bedroom.

She followed Captain Armati into the living room. Scout was a bowl of wiggles and jiggles when he spotted Millie. He pranced in a circle, which made Millie dizzy just watching him.

The captain picked Scout up and held him close before handing him over to Millie. "No. I am afraid I would roll over and crush him in my sleep," he admitted.

Which would be Millie's fear, too. Scout was so small, yet he was wiry. He was definitely a bundle of energy as he pawed at her cheek, licked her chin and tried to climb up her neck all at once.

Armati crossed his arms and watched the happy reunion. "How is the investigation going?"

Millie peeled her gaze from the dog and glanced at the captain. Of course, he would know all about it. He had probably already talked to Dave Patterson and knew that Millie had been in Courtney's room the night of her death. "The list of suspects is growing."

"Hmm." He picked up Scout's bag and held the door for Millie to follow him out. "We never had – uh – a death on board until the day you arrived and now we've had three right in a short amount of time."

Millie had to admit it did seem kind of like too much of a coincidence. First Olivia LaShay and now the young couple. She shot him a glance. Hopefully he didn't think *she* had anything to do with the murders.

Of course, she had been in the vicinity of all three incidents or had been the last person to see them alive, which would cause anyone concern. "I-uh. Yeah, it does seem like more than a coincidence." Millie shifted Scout and reached for his bag.

One of the employees was heading their way. Captain Armati patted Scout's head. "Behave yourself," he told the pooch.

Millie and Scout stepped into the hall. It was time to head down to the theater for the square dance class! Alison and Tara were already on stage, stomping around in their cowboy boots when Millie and Scout arrived.

Scout peeked his head out of the half window to catch a glimpse of the commotion. When he saw all the activity, he began to head butt the front of his carrier. Millie slipped her hand between his head and the carrier. "Scout! You're going to hurt yourself," she scolded him.

Alison stopped stomping. She strode over to Millie. "I heard a strange rumor about a pint size pup."

Alison twirled over in her western skirt. The skirt was cute. The material consisted of alternating strips of denim blue jean and red bandana. She dropped to her knees and put her hand inside to pet Scout. "Oh my gosh! He's adorable!" she gushed.

Her eyes sparkled as she looked up at Millie. "Can we take him out?" Millie didn't have the heart to say no. Plus, she wasn't sure who was more excited: Scout or Alison! She nodded.

Alison carefully unzipped the carrier and scooched back. She patted the stage floor. "C'mon out," she coaxed.

Scout hung back for a second, which surprised Millie. The dog was not shy! At least not around Millie. Finally, she was able to persuade Scout to leave his carrier. He wandered over to Alison and began to wag his tail, which shook his whole body.

Tara dropped down beside Alison. "This has to be the cutest Yorkie I've ever seen."

"Miniature Yorkie," Millie told them. "He belongs to Captain Armati."

Alison lifted her head and raised an eyebrow. "This is Captain Armati's dog? But how..." her voice trailed off.

"Ohhhh." Tara slowly nodded. "Captain Armati *likes* Millie," she teased.

Millie's face turned bright red. About the shade of the red in the bandanas on the girls' skirts. "My, my. I've never known him to take a liking to any of the staff." Alison waved her hands. "Millie's cast a spell over Captain."

"No!" Millie protested, "He just asked me to entertain his dog." It sounded lame. Even to Millie. Captain could have asked a hundred other people to do the exact same thing. People he knew better than Millie.

Tara picked Scout up and nuzzled him. "I heard Captain's wife died a few years back. His daughter has been hounding him to retire."

177

If Millie's face was red before, it was fire engine red now. Captain Armati was single. Just like Millie. Maybe he felt some sort of bond because they had both lost a spouse, in a roundabout way.

"Yeah. Not that some of the other women on board haven't tried to get Captain's attention. He never seemed interested." Alison's sharp blue eyes honed in on Millie again, which made Millie squirm.

Alison had heard bits and pieces of Millie's past. That her husband had left her unexpectedly and she applied for the job on a whim, not really expecting the company to hire her. Andy had told her that much.

She seemed like a nice enough woman. A bit on the grandmotherly side but it was a refreshing change from the competitiveness of some of the younger staff. Plus, adventure and mystery seemed to follow her around. Maybe the captain was attracted to that. Millie seemed - what was the word? Spunky!

She could see she was making Millie uncomfortable so she quickly changed the subject. "We have a skirt in the back I think you could fit into." She eyed Millie critically, which made Millie blush for the third time in a row. "You've got a little curve to you but that's a good thing."

Millie followed Alison to the back while Tara kept an eye on Scout. Actually, Scout was on the floor now and the two of them were chasing each other around, darting back and forth across the stage.

When Millie and Alison returned, Scout was back in his carrier and he didn't look the least bit pleased. But guests were starting to wander in and it was safer for Scout inside his carrier.

Even in his carrier, Scout managed to get a lot of attention as the passengers stopped by to pat his head and say hello. Scout was eating it up.

The square dance class was even more popular than the line dancing the day before, much to Millie's surprise. Millie knew most of the moves and before she knew it, she was stomping and twirling away. Millie was so caught up in the action; she didn't notice Captain Armati as he approached the stage.

When Millie caught his eye, she tripped on the tip of her boot and almost ended up in a heap on stage. The music finally ended. The captain was off to the side, talking to Scout. Millie tromped over to the two of them.

Captain Armati shifted his gaze from Scout to Millie. "I see Scout's having fun."

Millie nodded. "I didn't think he should be out for the dancing part but, yes, he's having a ball. He's like a little celebrity. All two and a half pounds of him!"

Captain Armati smiled for the second time, right at Millie. She nearly melted right then and there. Well, she didn't melt but her face turned a pale shade of pink.

"I thought I'd stop by to see how you two were doing." He patted Scout's head one more time and then glanced down at his watch. "I better go. I'm meeting with Detective Patterson to go over some things."

His smile disappeared and he gave Millie a look that she was beginning to understand. A look that said, please try to stay out of trouble or something like that.

Captain Armati strode down the center aisle and exited the theater. "Wouldja' look at that," Alison whispered. She lightly punched Millie's shoulder. "I think he likes you. I mean *likes* you."

"That's just crazy," Millie argued. "He doesn't even know me."

"Ever heard of love at first sight?" Tara asked. She tapped her cowboy boot on the wooden floor.

She began to sing an off-key rendition of "Love is in the air."

Millie put her hands to her cheeks and rolled her eyes. "Stop! You're embarrassing me!"

The guests still on stage had clustered off to one side. They were looking at Millie and she could only assume she was the topic of conversation. Millie wanted desperately to avoid that kind of attention!

Alison stepped to the center of the stage. "Back to work, folks. The show's over!"

The rest of the hour-long lesson flew by. Millie's heart was pumping and the exercise felt wonderful. Or maybe it was the thrill she felt at knowing the captain had made a special point to see her. Of course, maybe it was Scout.

Millie carried Scout to the backstage. She set him on the counter and slipped back into her work clothes. She hung the skirt on a hangar and slid the boots underneath the rack, right next to the others. She almost felt guilty; maybe she was having too much fun.

"You're the talk of the town – or should I say ship." Andy was standing behind her as she wiggled her foot into her work shoes.

"It does seem as if some sort of gossip is hanging over my head," she admitted. Millie pulled the ponytail holder from her hair and smoothed the locks back in place before rolling it into a tight bun.

She reached for the dog carrier. "What's my next assignment boss?" she joked. She secretly hoped it was trivia. Something a little more laid back, although the square dancing had been fun.

"Follow me." He motioned Millie back to his cubby. He settled in behind his desk. Millie sat across from him. She set Scout off to the side.

"I just got back from a meeting with Dave Patterson and Captain Armati. They are closing the internal investigation into Kyle Zondervan and Courtney Earhart's deaths. For all intents and purposes, it will be labeled a murder / suicide."

Millie's heart sank. She just didn't feel Courtney was the murderer. "What about the evidence?"

"Millie, it's just speculation because there really isn't any 'evidence.' The quicker the case is closed, the quicker we can get back to business. Giving passengers the best vacation possible."

He lowered his head and stared into her eyes. "That means you. I'm here to tell you on the record to stop snooping around and let it go."

Millie straightened her back. Her lips drew into a thin line. "Whose orders? Patterson or Armati?"

Millie wasn't sure if she liked either one of them anymore. Someone was trying to stop her!

He shook his head. "I'd rather not say."

Millie shot to her feet. She crossed her arms and glared down at Andy. "Well, I'm not going to stop!" She waved her hands in the air. "So they're just going to let a killer get away with murder."

"Authorities will take over once we get back to Miami." He shrugged. "They will do their own investigation."

Andy leaned back in his chair and lifted his hands. "Look. I'm siding with you. I think there's more to the story, but we have a job to do. That's why they pay us the big bucks."

Millie snorted.

"Maybe you could let Cat or Annette take over," he suggested. "You know. Kind of work behind the scenes. Let them take the lead this time."

Millie tapped her foot on the floor. On the one hand, she didn't want to bite the hand that fed her. On the other, she didn't like it when someone tried to tell her what to do. Of course, they were paying her to do a job, not solve a murder or murders.

Millie grudgingly admitted it was time to turn over the reins. Cat made the most sense. She had more freedom to move around the ship than Annette, who was pretty much stuck in the kitchen all day.

Her shoulders sagged. Millie was ready to admit defeat, but just this once. She decided to let it go.

Her decision lasted until the moment she exited the theater where she ran into Chloe Earhart.

"Oh! I've been looking for you!" the young woman exclaimed.

Millie cast a nervous glance behind her. She shifted Scout's carrier to her other hand. "Oh. What's up?"

Chloe grabbed Millie's arm and pulled her to the side. "I think I know what happened to Kyle and Courtney." Now Millie had every intention of turning over the investigation, but this was like a sign from heaven. It was like God dropping it right back into her lap.

She frowned. What harm could there be in at least listening to what Chloe had to say? "Let's head over to the..." She paused. They needed a nice quiet spot to talk. Somewhere off the beaten path. "Let's head up to the spa."

Chapter 16

The spa area was like a ghost town. One of the staff, who looked vaguely familiar, nodded to Millie. Millie had seen her around before but the spa staff worked for an outside company. They didn't work for the cruise line, which hopefully, meant that they had no idea what was going on.

The two settled on a bench seat to the left of the locker room. "What've you got?"

"This." Chloe pulled a piece of paper from her pocket. She shoved it into Millie's hand. "Proof that Courtney did not write the suicide note. This is her handwriting."

Millie frowned at the paper. She slipped her glasses on her nose then reached into her pocket to pull out her cell phone. She scrolled through the pictures until she reached the one she had taken of the note Courtney had supposedly written. Chloe was right. The handwriting was similar but not the same.

Of course, Courtney had been inebriated at the time of her death so it was possible she just didn't have the same steady hand she would've had if she had been sober.

Chloe pointed at the letter "T." "See how that loops around?" Millie nodded. "Courtney's "T's" were more rigid and taller.

Millie studied the "T." There certainly was a difference. She glanced at the young girl. "But that doesn't mean that Courtney didn't write this note."

"And what about the outfit that Courtney had on?" she argued. "We both know that wasn't the outfit she was wearing when she died. The outfit belonged to Melissa West."

Chloe had valid points and Millie agreed with her. It was just that she promised to butt out...to let it go. But this poor girl had just lost her twin sister! She sighed. "I don't know..." her voice trailed off.

Millie remembered the couple talking to the Wests as they exited the theater the night before. "How come you never told me there was another couple cruising with you?" Her eyes narrowed.

Millie had caught Chloe off guard. A flicker of uncertainty crossed her face, which she quickly replaced with a look of nonchalance. "You mean Justin and Kim Bain?" She waved her hand dismissively. "I barely know them. Courtney barely knew them."

Chloe paused as a thought occurred to her. "Kyle knew them. He went to college with Justin. He and the Wests. They all went to college together."

Millie was missing an angle here. It was almost as if it was right under her nose. So close, she couldn't get it. Couldn't put the pieces of the puzzle together.

Millie's eyes wandered to the clock on the wall. She remembered telling the Bain's, Maisie's parents, that she would bring Scout back to the same spot yesterday if they wanted to stop by and see him again. It was that time right about now!

She stood. "I have to head out, Chloe." She glanced around, making certain she was out of earshot. "Let me get back with you, okay?"

Chloe's eyes filled with tears. "I don't know where to turn." A lone tear rolled down her cheek. "You see, I have to do this for Court. I owe it to her."

Chloe pressed on. "Did you notice the door connecting Kyle and Courtney's room? The door that connected with Adam and Melissa West's room? Wouldn't that give them the perfect opportunity to sneak in and kill Courtney?"

Millie frowned. *And then there was Zack.*

Of course, the Wests *had* been up on deck when Kyle went over.

Millie looked down at Chloe's tear-stained face and her heart melted. She vowed then and there to do what she could to help Chloe. She couldn't imagine the heartbreak she felt over her sister's death.

On her way to the upper deck, Millie ran over the list of suspects in her mind. Adam and Melissa West since their cabin adjoined with Kyle and Courtney's room and Zack, who happened to be at the scene of Kyle going overboard.

Chloe, who was head over heels in love with Kyle. If she killed Kyle, why on earth would she kill her own sister - a twin sister at that? Then there was the mysterious couple – Maisie's parents.

With determined steps, Millie and her sidekick, Scout, wandered to the outer deck to wait for Justin and Kim Bain to make an appearance.

Chapter 17

Millie and Scout settled into the bistro table next to the sliding glass doors. It was the exact same spot that they had been in the day before. Millie's stomach grumbled. The square dancing had worked up her appetite.

Scout let out a low whine. Millie reached in to pet him. "I bet you're as hungry as I am." She glanced at her watch. If Maisie and her parents didn't show up in the next five minutes, Millie vowed to head inside for some food.

After that, it would be time to take Scout back to the captain's quarters. Her heart fluttered at the thought of seeing Captain Armati again. The flutter quickly flattened when she remembered someone was trying to squash her sleuthing. It didn't seem fair. Somehow, some way, she was going to solve these murders!

She quickly decided that after she dropped Scout off, she would stop by to see Cat. Maybe she could come up with an idea on how Millie could stay involved, yet still fly "under the radar."

Millie craned her neck and stared down the length of the deck. The couple had either forgotten about Millie or shown up earlier, before she got there. She hopped out of the chair. "C'mon Scout. Let's go get some chow."

She grabbed the carrier handle and pushed her chair in.

"Maisie! They're over there!"

Millie whirled around. Coming her way was Maisie and her parents! Millie pulled the chair out and plopped back down. She opened the carrier, lifted Scout and set him on the table.

Maisie made a beeline for the dog. "Pick up?" The little girl's innocent blue eyes begged Millie.

Millie nodded. "Have a seat, Maisie."

Maisie obediently sat in the seat across from Millie, who gently set Scout in her lap. "Scout."

"It-it's like a miracle," Maisie's father whispered hoarsely. He lowered to Maisie's eye level. "Maisie, would you like to get a dog – just like Scout?"

Her blonde head bobbed up and down. "Yes, Daddy. Just like Scout."

Maisie's mother burst into tears. She turned her back to the table. Long, painful sobs wracked her thin frame. Millie's heart was breaking. She turned to Maisie's father. "Will you watch them?"

His tear-filled eyes gazed into Millie's own. "Yes."

Millie put her arm around Kim Bain's shoulder and led her away from the table and over to the railing, out of earshot of the table – and Maisie. "I don't mean to pry, dear. I can see that something has traumatized your young daughter."

Millie turned back to gaze at Maisie and Scout. Maisie had set Scout on the bistro table and he was showing off. Maisie was giggling as she watched him bounce around in a circle.

"If you don't mind my asking – what happened to make Maisie stop talking?" She sucked in her breath and prayed the woman would spill the beans.

"There was a fire. Our house. It burned to the ground a few weeks ago." Her eyes slid to her young daughter and husband. "We barely made it out alive."

She turned to gaze out at the ocean. "I don't understand. Somehow, our smoke alarms - they never went off."

She wiped the tears with the back of her hand. "We almost died. We *almost* died. Our dog, Willie, didn't survive. Maisie was heartbroken. She stopped talking."

Her shoulders sagged. "We thought the cruise would help. Take her mind off losing Willie and bring her back to us."

"It didn't look like it was going to work." She went on. "Not until yesterday when she saw Scout."

The woman impulsively reached out and hugged Millie. "Thank you so much for sharing Scout with us. It has truly changed our lives. Saved our Maisie."

Now Millie was about to burst into tears. It was one of the saddest stories she had ever heard. Something about the story stuck in Millie's head. "Did the fire department tell you why the smoke alarms didn't work?"

Kim Bain shook her head. "No The house was so far gone, the alarms burned to a crisp. They melted down to nothing."

After the Bains left, Millie wandered inside with Scout. Kyle goes overboard. Courtney overdoses. The Bain's house burns to the ground. Was there connection? If so, what – or who – was it?

Millie and Scout filled a plate with goodies. A small sliver of roasted chicken for Scout. Roasted turkey, mashed potatoes and turkey gravy along with a side of corn and mouth-watering baked macaroni and cheese. Comfort food...the perfect thanksgiving dinner.

Millie glanced out at the bright sunny day. It was already October. Although it sure didn't feel like October in the Caribbean. Every day felt like the middle of summer. She wondered how she would feel when Thanksgiving rolled around.

Millie's first break wasn't until mid-February. This year would be the first holiday season she could remember that she wouldn't be with her children...her family.

She shoved the thought to the back of her mind and pressed on down the food line. She reminded herself that this job was an experiment. If it didn't work out, she could return to her dull, meaningless existence at the end of her contract.

Scout was shifting back and forth inside his carrier. He smelled all the goodies and Millie was certain he was as hungry as she was.

She plucked a plastic glass from a nearby stack and filled it with water from the fountain. Next, she grabbed a small saucer and headed to a corner table. Millie cut the chicken into tiny pieces and placed them in the center of the napkin. She placed the napkin inside the carrier.

Next, she poured a small bit of water in the bottom of the dish and set it next to the food.

Scout licked Millie's hand and then dug into his treat. Millie watched as the pint-size pup inhaled the goodies. Millie wondered if the captain had remembered to feed Scout before they left the bridge earlier.

He lapped up the entire saucer of water. Millie refilled the makeshift water dish. Scout promptly drank most of that and then stopped. He began to whine.

Millie's fork full of food was halfway to her mouth. That whine. It sound all too familiar. It was the sound Daisy used to make when she needed to go out. It was the sound of a pup who needed a potty break!

Millie's eyes darted around the room. There was no way Scout could take care of his business in here!

Millie shoveled several large bites of food into her mouth while Scout continued to whine. She needed to find a place for Scout to go – and fast. She threw her napkin on top of her dirty dishes and left them on the table.

She grabbed Scout's carrier and they headed for the door.

Millie was desperate. There was only one place she could think of that Scout would recognize. Millie took the stairs two at a time as she bolted to the top deck in the direction of the mini golf course.

At the edge of the course, she unzipped the bag and Scout darted out. He made a beeline for the second hole...the one with the plastic palm tree, its shiny green palm fronds blowing in the breeze.

Scout lifted his leg and watered the bottom. Next, he tried to tear up the turf as he pawed at the fake grass with his back feet.

Millie covered her mouth to stifle a giggle.

"Mommy, that doggy just peed on the side of that tree." A young boy was standing nearby, watching Scout in action.

Millie scooted across the fake grass. She lifted Scout, popped him into the carrier and darted off the deck.

"Sorry Scout. Next time I'll be sure to find a more appropriate place and plan for more frequent breaks," she promised.

"Ruff." Scout didn't seem to mind. He seemed peppy now, enjoying the open space of the mini golf course. It was like a built-for-Scout playground!

She grabbed the handle of the carrier. "I need to take you home."

Captain Armati was nowhere in sight when Millie and Scout stepped into the bridge. Millie wasn't sure if she was relieved or disappointed.

Someone Millie didn't recognize was studying the computer screen. It was a woman, her blonde hair pulled into a long ponytail that trailed down her back.

The woman turned when she heard Millie. She could have sworn the woman glared at her. She turned around, leaned a hip against the side of the massive screen, and crossed her arms.

"Ah. The infamous Millie Sanders." The woman spoke in a heavy accent. One that Millie couldn't quite place but guessed it might be Russian.

Millie stepped closer, her eyes reading the tag on the woman's shirt. "Ingrid Kozlov." Yeah, Millie was sure the name was Russian.

Millie tightened her grip on the carrier. "Is Captain Armati around?"

The woman gave a curt nod in the direction of the captain's quarters. "He's in there."

Millie nodded.

The woman glared.

Millie could feel the woman's eyes bore into her back as she and Scout headed down the small hall.

Millie softly tapped on the door and waited. There was no answer.

She knocked a second time, this time a bit louder. There was still no answer.

The hair on the back of Millie's neck stood up. Someone was watching her. She glanced back and Ingrid was directly behind the hallway, her eyes shot daggers at Millie.

Millie took a deep breath and rapped sharply on the metal door.

Captain heard it that time. The door swung wide open and the two of them came face-to-face. The captain's scowl quickly changed to a soft smile. "Millie. I was starting to worry."

He waved her in and quickly closed the door behind them. Millie's eyes scanned the room. He was eating lunch all alone!

"I-I'm sorry. I didn't meant to interrupt."

"No. It's okay." He shrugged. "I can eat in the dining room but sometimes, I would rather dine alone."

Millie knew exactly how he must feel. He must dread it even more than she did. What with having to suck up to the guests who were complete strangers and making small talk.

"I don't blame you." She handed Scout and the carrier to him and turned to go. "Tomorrow is island day. I have to be on the first shuttle to shore."

Captain Armati nodded. "I understand. Scout will miss you." He unzipped the carrier and Scout hopped out. "We'll see you the next morning?"

"Yes. Of course." She turned to go. She wasn't sure if Scout was going to miss her. She hoped that not only Scout, but maybe his master would miss her a little, too.

Millie avoided the gaze of the woman on the bridge as she made her way out. Millie was certain a set of shifty eyes followed her out.

Chapter 18

Millie's next stop was the lido deck. Her next assignment was supervising the ice carving competition. Something she'd never even seen before, let alone supervised. Sarah had told her it was cool so Millie was excited to watch the artisans in action.

Millie trailed behind the workers as they wheeled the large carts with blocks of ice out to the pool deck. Two young chefs followed behind, supervising the workers as they carefully eased the carts across the uneven deck.

Although the hottest part of the day was over, it was still a scorcher. As soon as Millie stepped outside, she began to sweat. Her brow, her neck, her armpits.

Sweat dripped down the back of Millie's neck and clung to her shirt. Whoever came up with an ice-carving contest in the tropical heat, in the middle of the afternoon needed to have their head examined.

Of course, the passengers didn't seem to mind the heat. But they were wearing swimsuits and shorts. Not long pants and thick cotton button down shirts.

She grabbed a paper napkin on her way to the sculpting area. She almost felt cooler as she envisioned flinging her body on the frozen chunks of ice.

It was fun to watch the two men compete and Millie was glad she was there to see it. One carved a sculpture of a dolphin breaking through a wave and the other, a mermaid sitting on a rock.

As she wandered back inside, she still couldn't believe they paid her for this, watching people having fun while having fun herself.

She thought about poor little Maisie and the trauma she'd gone through. The whole group of friends seemed to be plagued by a black cloud of death and disaster. What if someone had been trying to kill the Bains and they accidentally took out Kyle and Courtney instead?

She wondered how well Zack knew the Bain family – or the West family. Determined to find out, Millie headed to the other side of the pool deck. She could hear Zack's booming voice over the speakers. He was interviewing contestants for the Heart and Home series. It was a show where guests – married couples - competed against other married couples. Millie had never seen it but heard it was hilarious and a favorite among passengers.

Zack caught Millie's eye as he finished an interview. She stood off to the side and studied him. He was a nice looking young man. Kind. Funny. A good catch. The girls seemed to like him. He had dated poor Olivia. The young woman who had died the first day Millie boarded the ship.

Now there was poor Courtney. Also dead. Her brow arched. Two girlfriends. Both dead. Millie didn't want to suspect him but – wow - what an unusual coincidence.

Zack's voice echoed in her ear. "You got that look, Millie. I can see the wheels spinning in your head," he joked.

"They are," she admitted. "I was wondering if you knew any of the other passengers – the friends of Courtney and Kyle that are on board the ship."

He nodded. "Went to school with Justin Bain and Adam and Melissa West. Of course, Kyle was closer to them than I was. Kind of hard to keep up the friendships when you live on a cruise ship."

He had a point, which would eliminate him from suspicion on the fire that Kim Bain had told Millie burned their house to the ground. "Sad story about the little girl not talking. She's a cutie."

Millie had to agree. Maisie was adorable - and lucky to be alive, apparently. "What's your take on Kyle and Courtney's death?"

Zack's eyes watered. The thought of Courtney still hurt. Not that he loved her anymore. Still, he certainly didn't want to see her dead. "I can't imagine Courtney killing Kyle. Of course..." He trailed off.

"What?" Millie prompted.

"Well, Chloe confessed to me that Courtney and Kyle were having problems. That Courtney had just found out that Kyle was cheating on her," he blurted out.

Millie's brows formed a "V." Well, that made an interesting turn of events. "Do you know who it was?"

Zack shook his head. "I can only guess that was one of the things Courtney wanted to talk to me about. She was looking for advice. 'Course, we never got a chance after Kyle went overboard."

Millie studied Zack's expression. "Courtney told me someone had sent her a threatening note," she said. "Do you think there's a chance she didn't commit suicide and that someone killed her instead?"

He shrugged. "What about Chloe? Chloe was in love with Kyle. I think I mentioned that before."

Millie nodded. She remembered Zack telling her about the tattoo that Chloe had on her arm – the one with Kyle's name on it.

"Can you think of anything else? Any other clue that might be useful?" Millie had yet to talk to Adam and Melissa West, and now that the "powers to be" had told her to keep her nose out of an investigation that was, for all intents and purposes, over.

Zack shook his head. "Nope. If I do, you'll be the first to know," he promised.

Cat was her next stop. Cat would have to do a little sleuthing for Millie. Millie's heart sank when she saw all the passengers packed inside the gift shop. A sea day seemed to keep the shops and casino buzzing with customers and gamblers.

Millie waited until it cleared out before she headed to the back. Cat pushed back a piece of her beehive hairdo that had dropped down across her face. She tucked it behind her ear. "How's Scout?"

"Good. I took him back to the captain."

Cat's face fell. Millie hadn't realized how much Cat liked the pint-sized fellow. "I'll bring him back tomorrow," she promised.

Then she remembered it was private island day and she'd be on shore the entire day. "Oh. I can't tomorrow but the day after for sure."

Millie leaned an elbow on the glass top. "I need some help." She explained how she was supposed to stop snooping around Courtney and Kyle's death. She told Cat about the young couple and the fire.

Cat rolled her eyes. "You mean there are even *more* of them?"

"Don't worry about them. What I'm interested in is Melissa and Adam West. Their cabin was right next door to Courtney and Kyles and the cabins had a connecting door. Perfect access for someone to slip inside Courtney's cabin unseen." She lowered her voice. "Plus, Chloe, Courtney's sister, seems to think somehow Melissa West may be involved."

Cat's coiffed "do" bobbed up and down. She tapped a bright red nail on the counter. "I'm on it. What would you like to find out - other than where they were the night Courtney Earhart committed suicide?"

Millie waited for a customer to pay for their purchase before she answered. "If you can, find out who had access to their cabin, if they heard any strange noises coming from the cabin next door and if they think Courtney was capable of murder or suicide. You know...her general state of mind."

Cat frowned. "And make all of that sound like every day conversation."

A customer walked up, her shopping basket full of trinkets. *More like cheap junk made in China,* Millie decided. She smiled. The kids that were with the young woman looked excited with the treasures, which was all that really mattered.

Cat winked at Millie. "Will do."

Andy had given Millie a new assignment that day: head down to guest services and chat with the supervisor on duty. Find out if there were any grumblings or griping about the activities. Millie hoped not. She couldn't imagine guests not being happy with the variety of stuff going on every single moment of every day.

Guest services was a short walk and two floors down. Nikki, Sarah's friend, was behind the counter. She smiled when she saw Millie. "Hi Millie. I haven't seen you around much." Nikki leaned in. "Heard you're working the man overboard and suicide case."

Millie's smile faded. "I've been told to drop the investigation."

Nikki nodded. "So what brings you to my neck of the woods?"

"Andy asked me to check in. See if there are any customer complaints about activities and such."

Nikki shook her head. "Really. The opposite. Several have come up to mention that there's an adorable little dog on board. He's been seen on deck, at one of the dance classes - even up near the mini golf course."

Millie's face reddened.

Nikki burst out laughing. She lowered her voice. "I heard he was watering the green."

The look on Millie's face told her that was *exactly* what Scout had done. "Desperate times call for desperate measures."

"Well. No one complained," Nikki assured her. "Can you bring him by next time? I'd love to meet him."

Millie promised she would before she left.

She pulled her schedule from her pocket. There was one more activity on her schedule before she had a couple hours off. Millie slipped her glasses on and studied the paper. Ship-wide scavenger hunt. She folded the paper and shoved it in her pants pocket. This was something that would be right up her alley!

Millie bounded up the steps on her way back to the lido deck. A crowd – larger than the one that normally showed up for trivia – was

216

standing off to the side. She grabbed the microphone from a table nearby and switched it on. "Who's ready for a scavenger hunt?" Several whoops echoed from the enthusiastic band of sunburned passengers.

She pulled the now-familiar manila folder from behind the bar and studied the instructions. It certainly sounded easy enough. Hand the passengers a list of clues while she held onto the answers. Then wait for the first team – or person – to return with all the items.

Millie had a slight dilemma. She wasn't sure if she should have teams or an individual competition. She decided to let the participants pick. In an overwhelming decision, the passengers paired off in groups of four.

"Ready! Set! Open your list!" The groups studied their first clue and darted off toward the stairs. All of them took off except for one group. The group that was standing next to her, decided to start from the *bottom* of the list and work their way to the top. It was a smart move, guaranteeing they wouldn't collide with the other teams, all racing for the same thing.

She had a hunch she knew which team would take the gold, or in this case, the palm trees on a stick!

Millie studied the list and mentally checked off which ones she knew and which ones she didn't. It wasn't the piece of cake she assumed. She grinned. These folks were gonna get a little exercise on this scavenger hunt!

She wondered how Cat was doing and what she'd found out, if anything. Millie was bummed that she wasn't the one to talk to Adam and Melissa West!

Chapter 19

Cat watched the last shopper leave the store. It was time for her dinner break. Every day at 5:00 p.m. sharp, she locked the store and headed to the crew dining room. At 6:00, she would open back up and then stand around with nothing to do. Most of the passengers were either eating dinner or in the theater watching the show.

The store, like most stores on cruise ships, was in a well-thought-out location. It was on a direct path to one of the most popular areas of the ship: the theater and the casino.

Cat dimmed the lights and turned to lock the door. Out of the corner of her eye, she spied Adam and Melissa West across the hall. They were heading into the casino. Stumbling would be a more accurate description. Adam had a beer in his hand. Melissa was holding and spilling her martini.

Cat finished locking the door and edged her way into the casino, careful to make sure she was not in the West's line of vision.

She needn't have worried. They were sitting side by side at two slot machines; their backs were to Cat.

Cat glanced in both directions, then circled around the bank of machines until she was on the other side. She peered through the machines to make sure she was in the right spot.

Purser Donovan passed by. He gave her an odd stare, shook his head and walked on. *Great*, Cat thought. Just what she needed. Donovan spreading rumors she was a gambler!

Melissa was talking. Cat leaned in, her ear as close to the other side as she could get without actually wedging her skull in the narrow opening. She patted her up-do. That would definitely mess up her hair!

"Chloe said we're suspects," Melissa told her husband in a hushed voice - at least the woman thought it was hushed. Actually, it was quite loud, which was a good thing. The dinging of the machines made it difficult for Cat to hear her words.

"No Melissa. That's not true. Detective Patterson told Zack that the case was closed and they considered it murder and suicide by Courtney."

Cat's brows deepened into a "V." What on earth was Zack doing talking to the Wests? It wasn't his place to be discussing the case. She made a mental note to mention it to Millie.

"Well, I never thought it was Courtney," Melissa told her husband. "I think it was Kim. You know how she had that huge crush on Kyle and how mad she was when he told her to leave him alone."

Melissa went on. "I also think Kim set their house on fire, trying to get rid of her husband

221

and daughter. Why, I'd bet money she has a life insurance policy on him and Maisie."

Adam laughed nervously. "C'mon, Melissa. What person in their right mind would want to kill their own child?"

"That's what I mean, Adam. Kim isn't in her right mind."

Adam mumbled something else. Something Cat couldn't hear. She stayed a few more minutes but they had changed the subject and were now discussing Adam's bad grooming habits, which Cat did not want to hear. She popped out of the seat.

On impulse, she pulled a dollar from her pocket and stuck it in the slot. The machine looked lucky. Maybe it had something to do with the image of the woman on the front. Cat admired her slinky black outfit and awesome hairdo. *Elmira, Maiden of the Dark.* Anyways, she liked the looks of the machine.

She pressed the button to play one quarter. Nothing. She pressed the button again. Still nothing. There was a fifty-cent credit left in the machine. Cat pressed max and hit play. The lights on top of the machine started to blink and the machine began to make a dull beeping sound.

Dario, the casino's bartender, stepped over. "Cat! You won $500!" he told her.

Cat put her finger to her lips to shush him but it was too late. Adam and Melissa West popped around the corner. Melissa's eyes widened when she saw who it was. "Cat! I didn't know you were allowed to play in here."

Actually, Cat wasn't 100% sure she *could* play. Of course, no one ever told her that she couldn't.

She shrugged. "Beginners luck. The machine was calling my name."

She pressed the cash out button, grabbed the ticket and headed to the cashier. This sleuthing thing was starting to pay off!

Millie just happened to pass by the casino as Cat was at the counter cashing in her ticket. "Cat! I didn't know you liked to gamble."

Cat shoved the five $100 bills in her front pocket, grabbed Millie's arm and led her over to a small alcove off to one side. Cat sat down and patted the seat next to her. "Here. Sit."

Millie leaned in. The look on Cat's face meant she had something juicy. After she told Millie what she had overheard, she told her how the machine had looked lucky. Millie knew the exact machine she was talking about and the woman on the front – Elmira – looked a lot like Cat!

"So let me get this straight. Let's start with Zack. Zack dated Courtney."

Cat: "Check."

Millie held up a second finger: "Kyle Zondervan was engaged to Courtney but had previously dated Courtney's sister, Chloe, who was so in love with Kyle she had his name tattooed on her arm."

Cat: "Yep!"

Millie: "Now, on top of all that Kim Bain – Maisie's mother – was after Kyle."

Cat: "Bingo. Sounds like he was a real stud," Cat added.

Millie gave her a dark look.

Cat shrugged. "It's true."

"The only woman apparently *not* in love with Kyle was Melissa West."

Cat interrupted. "Or was she? I mean, maybe he rebuffed her advances. After all, their room was connected to Kyle and Courtney's."

"True." Cat had a good point. "But what about the husbands? If they found out their wives were hot for Kyle, wouldn't that be reason to want to get rid of him?"

Millie went on. "How does Courtney fit into all of this?" There were too many suspects! This guy had more reasons to have men hate him than Don Juan!

Earlier, Millie had seen a picture of Kyle and Courtney when she wandered up to the photo gallery to study the other couples. They all looked happy. None of them struck Millie as killer material. Kyle didn't look like he would have women swooning. Of course, Millie wasn't the best judge of that.

Cat glanced at her watch. "I need to go grab a bite to eat before it's too late."

The girls parted ways in the I-95 corridor with Millie heading to her room and Cat to the crew mess hall.

Millie stuck her key card in the slot and pushed the door open. There was a note on the floor. Millie had a moment of déjà vu. It reminded her of the time someone had slipped a threatening note under the door when she was investigating the Olivia LaShay murder.

Millie unfolded the note and slipped her reading glasses on. It was from Annette:

"Meet me in the kitchen. Stat! I have a plan."

Millie couldn't wait to find out what that might be. She made a pit stop in the bathroom before heading to the kitchen.

Annette was facing the revolving door when Millie popped in. She stopped what she was doing and met her on the other side of the gleaming stainless steel counters. "I talked to Cat. My theory is it was the couple next to Courtney's room. They had access and motive."

Millie cut her off. "What motive?"

Annette stuck her hand on her hip. "Why, that woman was messing around with Kyle."

"How do you know that?"

"Every good detective has hunches," Annette huffed.

Millie stiffened her back. The girls were hijacking *her* investigation! It wouldn't be long before Cat and Annette cut her out of the action!

Annette could see that from the look on Millie's face she was upset. "No, I mean. You've taught me so much already, I feel like a pro," she soothed.

Millie softened her stance. True. She was a good teacher.

"Anyways," Annette went on. "I baked a batch of special brownies." She winked. "You know – the ones that make you a little loopy. Loose lips sink ships and all that."

Millie frowned. "Great idea but how do we execute the plan?"

"How do they get to the room?" Annette tapped the side of her forehead. "Thinkin' girl. Always gotta be thinkin'."

"Anyhoo, I'm having Amit deliver a batch to their cabin, a special delivery, compliments of the captain."

"What if it backfires and they call the captain to thank him for the brownies?"

Annette frowned. "I never thought about that." She quickly dismissed it as a minor roadblock.

"Check this out." Annette stepped over to the counter and grabbed a plate. The plate was one that the kitchen used for room service. She flipped the plate over. There, in the center, on the bottom was a small black square. "It's a microphone."

Annette looked around before she reached over the back of the counter and grabbed a set of headphones. "We get the brownies into the room. After they eat some, they start blabbing. We have our killers' confessions."

She paused dramatically. "Voila! Case solved."

Millie took the headphones from Annette. "Where in heavens name did you get such a thing?"

The muscle in Annette's jaw twitched. "Let's just say, these came in useful in my previous life."

The look on her face made Millie hold back from asking the million questions that were now bouncing around in her brain. "Cool. But how do we – you know – listen in."

The twinkle was back in Annette's eyes. "That's the beauty of it. We sneak into Courtney and Kyle's cabin. We'll get great reception in there since it's right next door!"

Millie frowned at her friend. "That sounds a lot like breaking and entering." Although, technically, the room did belong to the cruise line, and they were employees. On top of that, Millie had done the exact same thing when she let Chloe snoop around inside.

Still, no matter how Millie tried to spin it, she was certain they could get in trouble. Not to mention the fact that Andy had already warned her to back off.

But if she told Annette she was out, then Annette and Cat would get to have all the fun. Millie crossed her arms defiantly. It wasn't fair! She nodded her head firmly. "Let me know when you're ready to go!"

Annette smiled brightly. "Good! I knew I could count on you." She looked around, then slid the headset into the cabinet and pushed it all the way to the back. "Amit will deliver the goods at 1950 hours."

"Which is?"

"7:50."

That would give Millie enough time to make her rounds, check in with Andy and assure him she'd be back to help with the Heart and Homes

231

show that started at 9:30. She hoped this wouldn't be a complete waste of time.

She didn't relish the thought of putting her job on the line based on Annette's "hunch." Maybe she could take Scout with her. She quickly dismissed the idea. What if he barked and blew their cover? On second thought, she decided she better leave him behind.

Maybe on their next investigation she could bring him along. Surely, a dog could be useful in the crime-solving business.

Chapter 20

The time seemed to drag by, although Millie stayed busy. She reported to Andy there were no complaints with guests. In fact, they seemed to love Scout. She told him the scavenger hunt had been a hit with the guests and that everything for the evening was on track for the couples show.

Andy interrupted her. "How's the investigation going?" Millie lowered her eyes. She wasn't good at lying. Not even half-truths. Instead, she kept silent.

She jumped when Andy slammed his fist on the table. "I knew it!" He leaned in. "Millie! I can see it in your eyes. What are you up to?"

"A little eavesdropping," she mumbled under her breath.

"Say it again, but louder," he commanded.

Millie sucked in a breath. "We're going to plant a small microphone in the room next to

Courtney and Kyle's old room and eavesdrop," she blurted out.

Andy raised his eyebrows. "This was your idea."

"Nope." She shook her head. "It's Annette's idea. She's the one that baked the special brownies."

Andy let out a harsh breath. "Special brownies?"

Millie shrugged. "Well, she called them truth serum brownies."

"And what exactly are in the 'truth serum' brownies?"

"Uh. I didn't ask. Honestly, I don't think I want to know."

Andy jumped to his feet so fast his chair tumbled backward and hit the floor with a loud thud. "She can't do that! She can't drug passengers!"

"She didn't say it was a 'drug,'" Millie argued, "I mean, she didn't use those words."

Millie held up her hands. "Look, Annette is not going to hurt anyone. Personally, I think she's just saying that. After all, where on earth would she get her hands on - you know – illegal stuff?"

Of course, maybe it was legal stuff. Legal in Jamaica. Also legal in some other foreign country that the ship just happened to visit...

It took Millie several more minutes but she finally calmed Andy enough to where he sat back down in his chair and didn't storm off to hunt Annette down. "You could go with us," she suggested.

Andy's eyes narrowed. Millie knew she had him! "Keep an eye on us. See how we operate."

"Make sure things don't get out of hand," she added.

Andy crossed his arms and leaned back in the chair. "I suppose I could."

Millie hopped up. "Great! We'll meet you out in front of cabin 4204 down on main."

Millie was on pins and needles as she waited to head down to the surveillance. Finally, it was time to go. Thankfully, no one was in the hall near Courtney's cabin.

Millie gave the door a gentle push. It slowly swung open. When she stepped through the door, she realized she was the last to arrive. Cat, Andy and Annette were already inside.

Annette gave her an odd look as if to say, "How did Andy find out?" but she didn't say anything.

Millie joined the group huddled around the small coffee table. A mini speaker was in the center. Headphones were lying beside it.

"Aren't you..."

"The speaker is hooked to the headphones so we can all listen in," Annette explained.

Millie nodded. She sat down on the edge of the bed and leaned forward.

"Amit dropped the special brownies off a few minutes ago. We haven't heard anything yet."

Just then, they heard a door slam. Cat whacked Millie's arm. "They're back," she hissed.

"Shush." Andy shushed them.

Cat gave him the evil eye.

There was giggling. "Don't do that." It was a female voice.

"Hmm and why not?"

"I wish I had some popcorn or snacks. Better yet, one of those brownies," Cat whispered.

There was more giggling.

Andy rolled his eyes. "I hope this doesn't become R-rated."

"Oh! What are these? It looks like room service dropped this off. There's a note 'Happy Anniversary.' It's from Andy Walker, Cruise Director. Now isn't that nice. Too bad it's not our anniversary."

Andy's head jerked around, his eyes widened and he glared at Annette. "You put *my* name on the brownies?"

Annette shrugged helplessly. "I didn't know what else to do!"

"Shhh!" Cat whacked Annette in the arm. "They're talking again."

"Mmm. These are delicious. Here, hand me another one." It was Adam talking this time.

"Too bad Courtney isn't here." A woman sniffled. "She loves brownies. I mean loved."

"Now don't start crying again, Melissa. You know how unstable she was."

"I know. That doesn't mean she killed herself."

There was a long pause. Millie shifted impatiently.

"Did you tell the detective the door between our rooms was open the night Courtney died?" Adam asked his wife.

"Why would I tell them that? Then they'd think we had something to do with Courtney's death."

"True," Adam admitted. "Last brownie. You want it?"

"No. It's yours," Melissa replied. "It sure is hot in here. We should turn down the air."

They heard a muffled thud.

"Whoa! Watch out, Adam. You almost fell on the coffee table."

Millie looked at Annette. "They're going to be okay, aren't they?"

"Yes. Yes." Annette assured them. "They'll be fine."

Andy wiped a nervous brow. "Yeah! My name is all over the stupid things. Thanks to Annette!"

"Stop arguing!" Millie spoke up. "We're missing it!"

"...why they don't question their own employee. You know, Zack was lurking around Courtney's cabin the other night."

"You don't think he killed Courtney." Melissa replied.

"I wish we had more of those brownies," she added.

Andy's mouth dropped open. "They were talking about Zack!"

The group waited a few more minutes. Soon they heard snores. The brownies must have knocked them out!

Andy abruptly stood. "Party's over."

He turned to Annette. "If anything happens to those two." He pointed next door. "I'm coming for you, Annette," he warned.

She gulped hard as she grabbed the headphones and small speaker. "Don't worry Nervous Nellie. They'll be just fine. They can sleep it off."

Millie wasn't worried about the Wests. She was worried about Zack!

"I guess it's time to have another chat with Zack," Andy told them.

Millie was sure Zack would be able to explain himself. The fact that he hadn't admitted being in the vicinity the night of Courtney's death was a bit of a worry.

Millie said a quick prayer for Zack, and Courtney and Kyle's families. She trudged behind Andy as she followed him back to his small office. The couples show would be starting soon.

The Heart and Homes show was hilarious. The place was packed and the show went off without a hitch. It was so much fun, Millie almost forgot about Zack.

She watched as Andy cornered him in the dressing room and then led him to his office. Millie closed her eyes. "Please, God. Don't let Zack be the murderer."

Millie wandered into the crew cafeteria. Her plan was to eat something quick and then head to bed. She would have to be up and ready early tomorrow to catch that first shuttle to the island.

Millie filled her tray with a scoop of rice and covered it with some sort of beef stew. She grabbed a slice of banana nut bread that looked suspiciously familiar.

She filled her glass with iced tea and headed to the tables. Sarah, Millie's roommate, and Sarah's friend, Nikki, were off in the corner. They waved Millie over. She hadn't seen the two of them together in what seemed like weeks but was really only days.

Millie slid her tray onto the table and pulled out a chair. She eyed the cheeseburger on Sarah's plate. Her mouth watered. It looked good and greasy. Just the way she liked them!

Sarah saw the look. She held out the burger. "Here. Try it."

Millie picked up the sandwich and nibbled the edge. It was delicious. "That's so good."

"So how's the investigation going?" Nikki asked.

"It has taken a turn for the worse," Millie admitted. She didn't go into details. Just told them there were too many suspects and not enough clues yet. Tomorrow was a new day.

Looking at the girls gave Millie an idea. As she sat there and made small talk, she hatched a plan. One to flush out the killer – or killers. It might be a bit of a stretch to pull off, but Millie was getting desperate - and they were running out of time.

Chapter 21

Millie was looking forward to her day on the island. She got to dress in clothes that were a bit more comfortable: Bermuda shorts and lightweight short sleeve shirt. Plus, it was fun watching the passengers when they caught their first glimpse of the island. It was almost like their own private island retreat. Away from the crowded, tourist filled islands with islanders hawking their wares.

Millie woke early. She was on a mission. She just prayed that all of the suspects got off. Otherwise, her plan might not work!

Millie stepped off the shuttle boat and headed to the nearest palm tree. Although it was still early morning, the sun was blazing hot. She pulled her cell phone from her pocket, turned it on and switched it to the pictures. The ones she had taken of Courtney's cabin the morning of her murder. There was one picture in particular she wanted to see.

She slipped her reading glasses on and tapped the small screen, making the picture as large as she possibly could. She studied the photo for several long moments. She closed her eyes and tried to memorize the photo. Ingrain it in the back of her mind. She did this several times, until she was certain she had it down pat.

She slipped the camera back in her pocket and made a beeline for Dario, the bartender who normally worked the casino. Since the casino closed while the ship stopped at the island, Millie knew he'd been assigned to the island, making his rounds, and serving the guests.

She pulled him to the side. "I need your help."

Dario tipped his empty beverage tray and slid it under his arm. "Yes, Ms. Millie. What do you need?"

"Receipts. I need to look at your drink receipts. Do you have a piece of scrap paper?"

Dario reached into his pocket and pulled out a small notepad and pen. He handed it to Millie. She scribbled the names of her suspects, minus Zack, on the sheet of paper and handed it back. "I need to see the signatures on these receipts."

He glanced at the list. "But what if they don't wanna order drinks, Ms. Millie?"

Millie grasped Dario's shoulder and stared into his eyes. "Now, Dario. Your job is to sell drinks, right?"

"Yes, Miss Millie."

"And I *know* that you are good at what you do." Millie laid it on thick. "You are one of the best bartenders on board the ship."

Dario smiled wide. "Yes." He puffed up his chest. "I sell them drinks, Miss Millie. Don't you worry."

Millie watched as Dario headed to the bar area. She could see Adam and Melissa West. They had just hopped up on two empty barstools at the island bar.

Dario walked over to the couple, leaned an elbow on the counter and started talking to them. Their backs were to Millie. She gave Dario the thumbs up and turned her attention to her job. It was time to make sure the steel drum band had the right playlist.

The day flew by. For the most part, Millie enjoyed the warm sunshine and tropical ocean breezes. It gave a bit of relief from hot, humid, stagnant air. She passed Dario on her way to make sure the lunch buffet was ready to go. "How's it goin'?"

Dario patted his pocket. "I have dem all, Miss Millie."

Millie couldn't wait to check out the signatures on the receipts. She had a gut feeling that finally, she might have something to go on, to lead her in the right direction.

The last of the guests boarded the 3 p.m. shuttle to the ship. A small army of crew remained on the island to tidy up and make sure it was ready for the next set of guests who were on another ship and scheduled to visit the island the next day.

She caught up with Dario as he worked at cleaning up the bar. He handed Millie a small pile of receipts. "They're all here, Miss Millie."

Millie lined the receipts on the bar. She plucked her phone from her pocket. Starting on the left, she studied each of the signatures carefully. Dario leaned over her shoulder.

Millie turned and patted his arm. "You managed to get the signatures for all of them!"

He nodded proudly. "Yes, Miss Millie."

She eliminated several of the signatures right off the bat. They weren't even close. But a couple of them were close. Millie snapped a photo of each of the receipts for reference. Something about the signatures was different.

She mulled it over for the next couple of hours as she finished cleaning and straightening. Finally, it was time to board the staff shuttle and head back to the ship.

A storm was brewing off in the distance and the small shuttle boat bounced up and down in the choppy waves.

Millie could hear the rumble of thunder in the distance. A flash of lightning touched the water a short distance from the ship. She let out a sigh of relief when the crew tethered the shuttle to the ship and slipped the plank onto the open deck.

Millie was one of the first off the ship. The cool interior air washed over Millie like a welcome breeze. The cool air must have cleared her foggy brain because it suddenly dawned on her that she knew exactly how to find the killer.

Millie headed up a flight of stairs to the photo gallery. Her heart raced as she frantically searched for the picture of Kyle and Courtney when they first boarded the ship. Her eyes scanned the rows of smiling faces. Actually, there were two pictures of Kyle and Courtney on display. The first one was of them as they boarded the ship. The backdrop was a picture of Siren of the Seas.

The second photo was a bit more casual. The picture had been taken as the ship departed Miami. Millie could see the city skyline in the background. There was one more thing about the photo - a very important clue that confirmed Millie's suspicions!

Millie headed back to her cabin. She studied the pictures of the receipts Dario had shown her one more time. Then she flipped back to the suicide note. Whoever had written the note had used a pen that was a bit on the leaky side. The writing was a little runny. It was the clue. A clue

251

that Millie desperately needed. After studying the suicide note, Millie was convinced whoever had written the note was left handed.

Millie had a plan. It would take a little luck and perseverance, and a little help from her friends.

Chapter 22

"So I need you to take note of how the suspects sign the receipts. Jot it down on a piece of paper and let me know," Millie told Cat. "Have they all been in here at some point in time?"

Cat scrunched up her nose. "I think so." She waved a hand. "Either way, we've having our 50% off sale tomorrow and *everybody* comes to that. I'm on it."

"Thanks Cat! I'm counting on you!" It had been a long day and Millie was whupped. The heat had made her even more tired and she wasn't necessarily a spring chicken, anymore.

Millie's last task for the day was to head up to the lido deck to check on the sail away party. Throngs of passengers crowded the area with their sunburned bodies.

Millie headed to the deck that overlooked the main pool. She stood at the rail and watched the island disappear. The storm clouds had moved away and the sun was just beginning to set. The view was incredible. It was God's magnificent creation.

The rail was crowded as passengers squeezed in with their cameras and drinks to toast the island and get one last shot. She glanced down the row. There, a few passengers to the left, was Kim and Justin Bain, Maisie's parents.

They were both holding drinks with cute little umbrellas. As they toasted each other, Millie studied their hands. They were both holding the drinks in their right hands. She let out a sigh of relief and tentatively crossed them off the list of suspects.

Millie headed down to theater. She hoped that Zack was working the bingo game that was about to begin. Her heart raced when she saw him at the front. He and another dancer, Felix, were carrying the bingo table to the center of the stage.

He waved when he saw Millie. She smiled and waved back. Millie slid into a front row seat and watched for several more minutes. Guests began to wander in, purchase the bingo cards and fill the empty seats.

Alison stood off to the side. She was in charge of selling the bingo cards. The line was long. Millie began to tap her foot on the floor as she grew impatient.

Finally, it was time to start the game. Millie's eyes followed Zack across the stage and over to the table and bingo cage. Her eyes grew wide as he reached down to grab the microphone – with his right hand! He turned the mike on and lifted it to his face. "Ready to win some cold, hard cash, ladies and gentleman?"

Millie popped out of the seat and headed down the aisle. Zack was off the hook!

That left Adam and Melissa West. And Chloe Earhart. Millie was closing in on a killer - or killers!

The casino was open when Millie walked by. She caught a glimpse of Dario out of the corner of her eye. He waved her over. "Miss Millie. Did you find the killer?"

Millie glanced around. "Getting close, Dario. Thanks to you," she whispered. He nodded, his face beaming brightly.

Millie exited the other side of the casino and nearly collided with Dave Patterson. "I've been looking for you," he told her.

Her heart fluttered a bit. Patterson's eyes pierced a hole in Millie. She was certain he knew she hadn't given up the investigation. Her eyes dropped to the floor. She quickly looked back up. She had always heard looking away was a sign that you were trying to hide something.

"Come with me." He didn't wait for Millie to answer. He led her down the stairs to Deck 2 and his office. There was no idle chitchat as they walked. Millie's steps started to drag. She felt as if she were heading to her own execution!

Patterson popped his key in the door and pushed it open. He stepped inside and held the door for Millie. He waved her over to the seat.

Millie pulled out the chair. It was then she noticed something on Detective Patterson's desk. It was bundle of blue material. A dress. The dress Courtney Earhart was wearing the night of her death.

Patterson rounded to the other side. He held up this dress. "Does this look familiar to you?"

Millie nodded. "Yes."

"This is not the dress Courtney was wearing when she died."

Millie shook her head. "No." She thought they had already gone over that. Maybe she missed something.

"Did Chloe Earhart give this to you?" Millie had told her to give take it to Patterson.

"No." He sunk down in the chair and dropped the dress on the top of the desk. "We searched Kyle and Courtney's room a second time and found it shoved in the corner of the closet. Buried, really. As if someone wanted to hide it."

He clasped his hands together. "You don't think Courtney committed suicide."

"No," Millie admitted. "I'm quite certain she didn't."

Patterson tipped back in his chair. "Why?"

Millie took a deep breath. "Look at the dress. Courtney was right handed. She spilled her drink down the right hand side of the dress."

"Go on."

Millie pulled her phone from her pocket. She scrolled to the picture of the suicide note. She tapped the screen and enlarged the photo then handed it to Patterson. "The suicide note was written by someone who was left handed. Courtney was not left handed. Although the writing is similar to Courtney's, the person who wrote the note dragged their hand through the wet ink, causing it to smear."

"How do you know Courtney Earhart wasn't left handed?"

Millie sucked in a breath. "I found a picture of Courtney and Kyle up in the photo gallery. They were up on deck before sail away – holding drinks – in their *right* hands."

Patterson picked up the phone and studied the image. "Hmm. But that doesn't mean she wasn't left handed."

"True," she admitted, "but judging by the way she held her drink and the fact that the stains were on the right side means she, at the very least, favored her right hand."

Patterson's eyes narrowed. Millie was right.

"I've got it narrowed down to three possible suspects." She held up her index finger. "One Chloe Earhart. Two Adam West. Three Melissa

West and only because I haven't been able to verify whether they are left or right handed. The rest in the group." She ticked off Zack, and Kim and Justin Bain. "Are definitely right handed."

Patterson touched his index fingers together and brought them to his lips. "Uh-huh."

Millie picked up her phone and dropped it in her pocket. "I should have answers on the rest before the day is out."

Patterson was studying her intensely. Her armpits began to sweat and her eyelid twitch. He was probably working out the details on how he was going to make sure the captain fired her.

He abruptly rose from his chair. "Let me know what you come up with."

Millie jumped from her chair and bolted out the door. She could feel his eye bore into the back of her skull. She was tempted to turn around and stick out her tongue – but that did not seem particularly professional so she resisted the urge.

That 60's Show was the headliner for the two evening theater performances. Millie stood off to the side and watched the first set. Zack was in his glory as he danced and spun around the stage. Millie's chest puffed with pride. He was such a good kid. The fact that he wasn't a killer didn't hurt, either.

After the show, she stopped by Cat's shop, hoping she had found something. The place was deader than a doornail. All of the guests were either at the show or in the dining room if they had reservations for the second seating.

She stepped inside. "How was business today?"

Cat groaned. "It was pure chaos. You'd have thought we were giving stuff away!" Millie had to admit she looked a bit on the frazzled side. Her normally meticulously coiffed and perfectly centered beehive hairdo was a bit off kilter. "Busier than a mosquito at a nudist colony."

Millie chuckled.

Cat placed a hand on each side of her hairdo and shifted it back in place. "There. That's better." She snapped her fingers. "I'm centered again."

"Oh! I got my handy dandy little list right here." Cat lifted the ladybug paperweight on top of the counter and grabbed a small sheet of paper. She handed it to Millie. "The results."

Millie slipped her reading glasses:

Adam West. Right hand.

Melissa West. Right hand.

Chloe Earhart. Right hand.

Kim Bain. Right hand.

Justin Bain. Right hand.

Millie's heart sank. This wasn't going to work. All of them were right handed! The killer was left handed. Millie crumpled the list. "They're all right handed. The killer – the one who wrote the suicide note – was left handed."

She was back to square one...right where she started!

"Maybe the killer was so good, he *pretended* to write it left handed," Cat theorized.

Millie shook her head. The killer wasn't that good, unless they were a professional, which she seriously doubted.

Millie was depressed. She thanked Cat for the list and trudged out. She was so sure the killer was left handed!

Millie headed down below. It was time to give Dave Patterson the bad news. Luckily, she caught Patterson in his office. The look on Millie's face said it all. She plopped down in the chair.

"You look like your best friend just died."

Millie let out an exaggerated sigh. "Almost! All of the suspects are right handed."

Patterson picked up his pen and tapped it on the desktop. "So your investigation is at a standstill."

Millie tugged on the corner of her ear. "This is the hardest case I've ever had to crack."

Patterson grinned. "This is only the second case you've ever had," he pointed out. "That I know of, anyways."

Patterson had a point. Still, she was so certain. So sure she could catch the killer red handed. Or in this case, left handed.

Patterson began drawing small circles on his notepad. "What's the plan now?"

Millie groaned. "That's why I'm here. I mean, you're the paid professional!"

"True," he admitted. "Your enthusiasm makes up for your lack of experience. I have to admire your tenacity."

Patterson stopped drawing on the pad. He gave his full attention to Millie. "I know you want to believe there's something more to the case. But the fact is, Courtney Earhart killed Kyle Zondervan. Consumed by guilt, she decided to take her own life."

Maybe Millie was grasping at straws. Trying to make something out of nothing. She wondered if she'd ever mentioned Courtney's confession about being threatened. "Courtney said that she had been threated. That she felt her life was in danger."

Patterson leaned forward and listened intently. "Did Courtney show you the threatening note she supposedly had?"

Millie shook her head. "She was so far gone, I was lucky I was able to get her back to her cabin before she passed out. That is another reason I don't believe she had the ability to write the note or take those pills."

"And change her clothes," she added.

"What if she sobered up? It was several hours, late morning before the cabin steward discovered her body."

"So you're going to let the case stay as it is," Millie said.

Patterson stood. "I don't have much of a choice. Unless the killer decides to come forward and confess. We're running out of time. A couple more days and the passengers disembark and if there is a killer, he or she walks off."

Chapter 23

Millie shuffled back to her cabin. She was tired and hungry. She was so exhausted that tired outweighed hunger. Last but not least, she was discouraged.

The only silver lining was that Zack was off the hook. Not that she ever really believed he could be a killer anyways.

Millie decided to skip dinner and go straight to bed. Which would have worked out fine if Captain Armati hadn't been standing outside her cabin door, waiting for her.

He smiled when he caught sight of Millie. She patted her windblown hair, certain she must look like a wreck. She sure felt like a wreck.

Her heart sank. She was probably in big doo, doo now. He probably heard about the brownies. Or maybe someone had spotted Scout watering the palm tree on the mini golf course. Or it could've been...

"Hello, Millie. Did you have a nice day on the island?"

She let out the breath she'd been holding. Judging by the tone of his voice, she wasn't in trouble after all.

Her heart skipped a beat. Maybe something had happened to Scout!

"It was a nice day. Hot but nice," she replied. "Is Scout okay?"

The captain nodded. "Scout is fine. I think he missed you, though. He watched the door all day."

Millie eased her tired body against the hall wall. "Then I can take him out tomorrow?"

The captain nodded. "Follow me." He started walking. Millie pulled herself upright and followed along.

"Have you eaten dinner yet?"

Millie shook her head. "I was thinking about skipping it. You know, the heat and all." *And the failed investigation*, she added silently.

He stopped, put his hands behind his back and nodded thoughtfully. "You're not hungry?"

Her stomach grumbled in protest. The captain? Dinner? Her appetite was making a strong comeback. "Well, I guess I probably should eat something. I always told my children never to go to bed on an empty stomach."

"That's true. I'm heading to dinner myself. Would you care to join me?" His eyes crinkled kindly.

A lump lodged in her throat. "That would be nice," she squeaked. She cleared her throat and tried again. "That would be nice."

"Good!" He nodded. "Scout will be thrilled to see you."

He started walking again. "How does surf and turf sound?"

Lobster was a luxury. Something that Millie had tried only a handful of times. "It sounds great, although I've only had it a couple times," she admitted.

They were in front of the elevator now. The captain pressed the button. When the door opened, he motioned Millie in first. She looked down at her crumpled, sweaty shorts, wrinkled shirt and then over at his crisp, clean uniform. "Maybe I should change first."

"I think you look fine just the way you are," he assured her.

Millie felt the familiar burning sensation on the outer part of her ears and knew that right about now, they were fire engine red.

If Captain Armati noticed, he was too much of a gentleman to comment.

Millie was relieved when the elevator reached the 10th floor. She hadn't dared mention her aversion to elevators!

It was a short walk from the elevator to the bridge. Millie smiled at Staff Captain Vitale as she followed Captain Armati to the center of the bridge and down the small hall leading to his private quarters.

The captain punched in the code on the key pad and pushed the door open. Millie followed him in.

Dusk was beginning to set and the interior cabin glowed in a soft light. Her pulse started to race.

A small shadow darted out from underneath the table and ran right into her. It was Scout! Millie leaned down and picked up the wiggling bundle. He was moving so much, Millie could hardly hold onto him!

He licked her face, her hands, anything his small pink tongue could reach. Finally, he calmed down long enough for Millie to put him back on the floor. He promptly circled her several times.

"Wow! He doesn't even do that when I'm gone all day!" the captain joked.

"Dogs and kids. I know how to attract 'em," Millie answered wryly.

Millie brushed her hands on the front of her pants. Her eyes traveled to the table tucked off in the corner. A crisp, white tablecloth covered the table. In the center was a tall silver candleholder with a long tapered candle inside. Lit and giving off a romantic glow.

Millie's ears started to burn again and her eyelid began to twitch.

The captain handed Millie a wine glass. "Care for a glass of wine?"

Millie wasn't a drinker. A glass of wine on a special occasion was the extent. But she was nervous and the wine might help calm her nerves.

Next to the table was an ornate silver wine cooler. Inside the cooler was an open bottle of wine. She nodded.

The captain filled two glasses and handed her one. He motioned toward the balcony. "We should enjoy what's left of the day."

He slid the slider door open and waited for her to step out first. Scout was right on their heels.

Good. A chaperone, Millie thought to herself.

They settled against the railing and Millie sipped the wine. It went down smooth. Too smooth. "This is a nice wine. What is it?"

"Santa Cristina Chardonnay." He swirled the wine in the glass before taking a sip. "It's Italian."

He lifted his glass. "A toast."

Millie raised her glass. "A toast."

"To the ocean and adventure," he said.

Scout was nibbling on her ankle. "And Scout," she added.

They tapped glasses and she took another sip.

"Are you still enjoying life on board?"

Millie nodded. She *was* enjoying life on board the ship. She loved the adventure, the activities, her new friends, and the detective work.

She snuck a quick glance at the captain. *Romance.*

"Yes. This is so different from anything I've ever known," she confessed. "Every day is new and exciting."

He slowly nodded as he stared out at the water. He wondered if the ocean would get in her blood like it had his. Of course, he knew even when he was a young boy that he wanted to sail the seas. He never wanted to play with action figures or toy trucks or trains. It was always the boats.

He had grown up near the water, in the small village of Bertoli, on the Mediterranean Sea, where he would stand at his bedroom window for hours and watch the larger boats as they sailed by the small village. He loved the smell of the ocean air, the sound of crashing waves, wondering what lie in the bottom of the deep blue sea.

Niccolo, or Nic as his family and friends called him, had been married to his wife for 40 years before she died in a car accident.

Nic had been at sea when it happened. When the news of her sudden death reached him, it took long, agonizing days for him to make it home. He made it just in time for them to put her in her final resting place. His deepest regret was not having the chance to tell her good-bye.

Captain Armati's daughter, Fiona, had been angry with him for months. Angry that he was not there for her when her mother died. Finally, slowly, her anger faded. But Nic had made a solemn vow to himself. To never marry again.

Lisa was a wonderful wife. She was irreplaceable and always in his heart.

Nic gave himself a mental shrug. He hadn't meant to go there...not tonight.

He caught Millie's eye. The woman intrigued him. She was different. Different than his other crew. Different from any other woman he had ever met. She had spunk. He liked that. He wondered what made her tick. Maybe it was because she was an American.

Millie tucked a stray wisp of hair behind her ear and looked away. She knew he was studying her.

"What is your favorite assignment so far?"

Millie turned back. She squinted her eyes. "Hmm. I'd have to say the dance lessons are fun. Of course, I've enjoyed hosting the trivia. But then there was the scavenger hunt the other day." She shrugged. "It has all been fun."

Nic laughed. "Okay. Maybe it would, uh, be easier if I asked you what you *haven't* liked about your job so far."

Millie's eyebrows drew together. There wasn't too much she hadn't enjoyed. Other than not being able to solve the stinkin' murder, but she wasn't about to bring that up!

"Hmm. Maybe the tiny quarters," she admitted.

"Ahh." He nodded. "Well, there isn't much I can do about that."

They heard a light tap on the outer door.

"That would be the arrival of our dinner."

Millie followed him indoors. She waited off to the side while the steward pushed a covered cart to the table. The cart was loaded with trays! A sterling silver half-moon cover concealed the contents of each plate. It was a very elegant presentation.

The captain pulled out a chair and motioned for Millie to have a seat. He pushed her chair in and took the seat across from her.

"Shall I stay?" The young man asked.

The captain shook his head. "You can serve the first course and then you're free to leave. We will serve ourselves."

The man lowered into a small bow and backed out of the room. Millie was 100% certain that the rumor of the captain dining with the assistant cruise director would spread like wildfire through the ranks.

That is, unless, of course, the captain entertained women on a regular basis. Then it would be ho-hum. Millie frowned at the thought.

The first course was a small tossed salad. Along with the salad was a selection of dressings. Millie picked the ranch and scooped a small spoonful over the top of her salad.

She lifted the corner of the cloth that covered the breadbasket and studied the contents, searching for a piece that wasn't too awful chewy – one that wouldn't stick in her throat. She settled on a slice of rye.

Millie had always prayed over her food. She clasped her hands together and bowed her head. Much to her surprise, the captain did the same. She whispered a small prayer and asked the Lord to help make sure she didn't embarrass herself in front of him.

When she lifted her head, he was watching her, a small smile on his lips. "Ah. Now I know what is so special about Mildred Sanders. You are a praying woman."

Millie blushed. Just a teeny bit this time, and nodded her head. "The Lord has been good to me," she said simply.

"And to me, as well." He tilted his head to the side. "Have you been to chapel and met Pastor Evans?"

Millie spread a thick layer of creamy butter on top of her bread and nibbled the edge. "Yes. Last Sunday. It was a lovely service."

It reminded Millie that tomorrow was Sunday and she had the morning off.

She slid the butter dish across the table.

Captain Armati picked a crusty baguette. He broke the piece in half and reached for his butter knife. "I would go. Occasionally I do go. Most Sunday mornings are port days and I have to be on the bridge to guide the ship to dock," he explained.

"But tomorrow. Perhaps I will go," he added.

Millie finished her salad and set the plate, along with her fork, on the lower level of the cart.

The captain pushed back from his chair. "No. You are my guest. I'll take care of that."

He nestled his empty salad bowl inside of her bowl and set them on the cart. Then he lifted a covered dish from the tray. He uncovered the dish and set it in front of Millie.

Millie studied the contents. It was a small bowl of gazpacho soup. One of Millie's favorite.

"I hope you like tomatoes," he told her.

Millie loved tomatoes. And peppers. And cucumbers. It made her think of the large garden she normally planted in the spring. "This is my favorite," she gushed.

Pleased that he had made the right selection, Captain Armati set the second bowl of soup on his side of the table. "Mine too," he confessed. "I could probably eat this every day."

When they got to the main course, surf and turf, Millie looked down at the lobster tail in dismay. She frowned, not sure how to crack the hard shell.

The captain sensed her hesitation and quickly reached over to take her plate. "May I?"

Millie nodded. "Have at it."

With expert precision, he plucked the fins off and then twisted the body. Using the tip of his knife, he pushed the meat through the shell. It landed in the center of the plate.

"Well, it's a good thing I didn't attempt to do that," she muttered. Visions of flying lobster crossed her mind.

He handed the plate back. There was a round tin of melted butter. She cut a small piece of lobster and dipped it in the tin. It was a bite of pure paradise. She rolled her eyes. "This is delicious!"

Nic repeated the same steps for his lobster and then dropped the shells and tail into a bucket. He cut a large piece and drizzled butter over the top. He cut a smaller section and took a bite. "Yes. Very good," he agreed.

The dinner was the nicest meal she'd had on board, which may have had something to do with the company she was keeping...

There were a few times, she caught him cutting small pieces of his porterhouse steak and then sticking his hand under the table to feed Scout.

After dinner, he poured two cups of coffee and uncovered a tray of tempting bite size desserts. "Shall we finish out on the balcony?"

Millie balanced the dessert plate and opened the slider while he carried the carafe of coffee and two cups. He set the dishes on a small table between the chairs. It was perfect for the space.

Millie poured a dash of cream in her coffee and took a sip. "Thank you for inviting me to dinner. It was lovely, Captain Armati."

"Nic. Please. At least in private, call me Nic."

"Nic." It rolled off Millie's tongue. His name was fitting.

They chatted about home and their children for a long time. Millie glanced at her watch. It was getting late. She needed to get to bed if she planned to get up for church in the morning.

"You must be tired," he told her.

And smelly, she thought. She nodded. "Yes. Tomorrow will be a busy day."

Her mind wandered back to the investigation, or what was left of it. She had all but given up on it.

She followed the captain back inside. Scout was waiting by the door, as if he somehow knew she was getting ready to leave. "I'll see you after church," she promised.

Her only answer was the lick of his tongue on the side of her face.

The captain led her out, through the bridge and opened the outer door. He gave a small bow as Millie stepped into the hall. "Thank you for a lovely evening."

Captain Armati smiled. "Yes, it was lovely. Thank you, Millie, for joining me." He didn't wait for a reply. Instead, he slowly closed the door as Millie walked away.

Millie floated back to her cabin. The evening had been almost magical.

Chapter 24

Millie unlocked her cabin door and stepped inside. She wondered if she would even be able to fall asleep.

Sarah was nowhere in sight. Millie quickly brushed her teeth, washed her face, pulled her pajamas on and crawled into bed. It was only 10:00 p.m. but Millie was whupped. She whispered her prayers and pulled the covers to her chin.

Millie had just dozed off when her radio, which she forgot to shut off, began to crackle.

"Miss Millie. Are you there, Millie?" It was Dario.

She switched on her night light and crawled out of bed. The radio was on the desk. She almost didn't answer but decided to find out what Dario wanted. It was unusual for him to radio her and he sounded excited.

She turned it up and pressed the talk button. "Go ahead, Dario. I'm here."

"Miss Millie," he said breathlessly. "I have news." He lowered his voice. Millie could barely make out his words. "I have news on the investigation. You'll never guess what I just found out."

Millie was torn. Should she put her clothes back on and find out what "news" Dario had that sounded so promising? Could it wait until morning?

Millie knew there was no way she would be able to sleep. No way that she could. "I'll be right there. Where are you?"

"In the casino, Miss Millie."

Millie slipped on a clean pair of shorts and t-shirt. She grabbed her flip-flops from the shelf and shoved her feet in.

She studied her reflection. At least she didn't have bed head. Millie slipped her lanyard with her ID and room key around her neck and headed out the door.

Her mind was whirling. What on earth could Dario possibly have stumbled upon that would move the investigation forward? He seemed so excited.

The casino was packed. Dario was pacing the floor when Millie stepped inside. Millie had never seen it this busy. Of course, she didn't spend much time on this floor, especially at night. She spent most of her evenings in the theater.

When Dario spied Millie, he hurried over. "What've you got, Dario?"

"Well, you know how you look for someone that write with their left hand? Someone that was on your list?"

Millie nodded. "But everyone on my list was right handed. We checked."

"Yes." Dario's head bobbed up and down. He pulled out two drink receipts. He handed the first

288

one to Millie. He pointed at the signature. "They sign this using right hand."

"Okay."

He laid the second receipt on top. "This one. They sign using *left* hand."

Her eyes widened. "They're ambidextrous."

Dario grinned. "They sign using *both* hands."

Millie's eyes traveled to the top of the receipt and the name printed there. She sucked in a breath and held it. "Oh my gosh!"

The receipts fell from her loosened grip and fluttered to the floor. She picked them up and shook them in her hand. "Still, this isn't concrete proof that we have the killer." She folded the receipts in half and handed them back to Dario.

"We need to trick them. Make them think we have evidence and hope they confess." It might just work. Millie was running out of ideas.

She patted Dario on the back. "You're sharp, Dario."

Dario puffed up his chest. "I join your team." His eyes shot up. "You need someone like me."

He leaned forward and whispered conspiratorially. "I love that TV show. What is it? Detective Gumbo!

Millie grinned. Detective Gumbo. She used to love to watch the old reruns. Back in the day when she had a TV - and a house. Yeah, the show was great but now she was living it!

Millie slowly walked back to her room. She had only a couple more days to get a confession. Time was running out. Tomorrow morning was church and she had to work in the afternoon. She needed to come up with a plan and fast!

Chapter 25

Millie, Cat and Annette sat together at the morning church service. Millie had just enough time to tell them they had a good lead on the killer when Pastor Evans started the service. His message was one of patience. Not one of Millie's strong suits. In fact, some people described her as downright impulsive. The key verse was:

"Be joyful in hope, patient in affliction, faithful in prayer." Romans 12:12 (NIV)

After the service ended, the girls wandered down to the crew cafeteria for brunch - if you could call it that. It was a hodgepodge selection of food: eggs, bacon and toast. They also had chicken tenders, wraps and sub sandwiches.

Millie was in the mood for breakfast. Something she normally didn't get a chance to sit down and eat because she was working. She was lucky most mornings if she had time to grab a slice of toast and a cup of coffee.

The girls headed for a table in the corner. Cat set her tray down and slid into the open seat. "What've you got?"

Millie told them what Dario had discovered.

"We should add him to our team," Annette suggested.

Millie had to agree. Dario's position as bartender gave him access to many of the ship's passengers. He spent most of his days working in the casino but he occasionally worked on lido and he was always on the island.

"He offered," Millie told them. "I think he would be perfect!"

Cat picked up a fry, dipped it in ketchup and popped it in her mouth. "What's the plan?"

"I think if we allude to the fact that the investigators have evidence and are about to make an arrest."

"So you're going to lie?" Annette was surprised Millie would use this tactic.

"Oh no." Millie shook her head. "Not a lie. Just kind of put it out there like..." She paused. She didn't have the exact wording yet. This detective stuff was still new to her and Millie was pretty much flying by the seat of her pants. "I'll find a way to wheedle it out."

Scout was waiting for Millie when she got up to Captain Armati's apartment. The captain himself was nowhere in sight. The woman in the bridge told her he had stepped out. The captain had given Millie the code to his door the night before so Millie entered the code and let herself in.

It felt odd being alone in the captain's personal quarters, although she wasn't really alone. Scout dashed to the door and pranced in circles around Millie's feet.

The first thing Millie did was take Scout out to his potty pad on the deck before she grabbed his carrier and they let themselves out of the apartment.

Scout was so excited to be out and about, he wiggled all around in his carrier. Millie had to use both hands to hold him.

She had less than an hour to round up her suspect and get a confession. After that, she had to report to Andy's office for her afternoon assignments.

Millie knew there was a 50/50 chance she would find her suspect on the upper deck, soaking up the rays near the VIP area. *Returning to the scene of the crime,* she thought.

Millie was in luck. There, sitting in one of the padded lounge chairs, was Chloe Earhart. She looked up when Millie wandered over and blocked her sun.

Millie stuck her hand on her hip. The girl was too pretty to be a killer. Maybe she was blacker than coal on the inside. Millie grabbed the edge of a nearby chaise and dragged it close.

Chloe set her book on her lap. "I was looking for you earlier, wondering how the investigation was going. We're running out of time," she pointed out.

Millie thought the exact same thing, which was why she was there!

Millie set Scout's carrier on the deck and unzipped the door. He stepped onto the deck and began to sniff the chair. "Stay close," she warned him.

Scout looked back. Millie could almost swear that he nodded.

She turned her attention back to Chloe. "Oh! Great! Security is about to make an arrest." This, technically, might be the case if Millie could just get a confession!

She watched as Chloe's hand went to her throat. Her other hand tightened on the pages of her book.

"Th-That's great news!" she stuttered. "Do you know who it is?"

Millie looked at her solemnly. "Yes. As a matter of fact, I do."

The color drained from Chloe's face. She slid her sunglasses on top of her head. "Who is it?" she whispered.

Scout was back. He stared at Millie and began to whine. She picked him up and set him on her lap.

"We both know who the killer is, don't we, Chloe?"

"I-I don't know who it is. That's why I asked you to help me."

Millie rubbed Scout's chin thoughtfully. "Courtney was right handed. Someone who was left handed wrote the suicide note. Or, quite possibly ambidextrous. You know, someone who can write using both hands."

Millie went on. "Last night in the casino, you ordered two drinks from the bartender. You signed one with your right hand. The second one, you signed with your left."

Millie moved in for the kill. "Why did you kill your sister, Chloe? Did you hate her that much? Was it because she stole your boyfriend?" Millie glanced down at Chloe's arm. The arm that had Kyle's name tattooed on it.

Chloe's mouth set in a straight line. She closed the book and sat upright in her chair. "She killed him. Courtney killed Kyle. She took him away from me! She had to die."

Now it was Millie's turn to be shocked. Courtney had killed Kyle? Why would she do that? What could make Courtney so angry that she pushed her fiancé, Kyle, overboard?

Millie shifted her gaze to the girl sitting across from her. Chloe was ready to talk.

Luckily, they were sitting alone in the chairs. The nearest passenger was several feet away.

"Kyle and Courtney had been fighting even before they got on the cruise ship. Kyle wanted to postpone the wedding. He confided in me that he was having second thoughts, that all they ever did was fight."

Millie had to wonder if it didn't have something to do with all of the women that were fawning over him.

"Courtney never admitted it, but I think Kyle told her he was still in love with me. That was the real reason he didn't want to marry her. When she found that out, she became so enraged she pushed him overboard. If she couldn't have him, no one would."

"So you killed her."

Chloe lifted her arm. The tattoo was large — and clearly visible. It was colorful. Pink and blue. Kyle's name was blue. The heart around it was pink. "We were meant to be together forever and Courtney ruined it."

The tears began to roll down Chloe Earhart's cheeks. "Now I don't have Kyle or my sister and it's all Courtney's fault."

Millie shifted in her chair. It was Courtney's fault that her sister had killed her? That was so messed up!

"So when Courtney confessed to you she had pushed Kyle over the rail, you decided she deserved to die," Millie prompted.

"Only after the doctor. What was his name?"

"Gundervan."

Chloe nodded. "Courtney told me she pushed Kyle in a fit of rage. When Doctor Gundervan told me Kyle was dead, I began to plot how I could get rid of Courtney. It was the only thing that helped me deal with the grief."

"Revenge," Millie interjected.

"Exactly. Since Court and I had similar handwriting, it was easy to write the note. I let myself in her cabin using Kyle's key. When I got inside, she was so drunk; she had passed out on the bed."

Millie frowned. That must have been right after she left.

"So I woke her up and told her to change. I told her that the doctor had been wrong and Kyle was still alive."

"I snuck into Melissa and Adam's cabin through the connecting door and grabbed the dress from their closet. We changed Courtney's outfit and then I grabbed the pills from my bag. I told her to take a few to calm her nerves and then I promised her that we would go get Kyle."

"She was so drunk, she kept gagging on the pills," Chloe scoffed. "Finally, she just passed out so I took one of the pillows from the bed and..."

"You suffocated her?"

"Yeah." Chloe shrugged. "I thought it would be harder than that."

"So you decided to stay on board the ship and make sure that Melissa West was blamed for her death: the dress, the unlocked door between the cabins."

An evil grin spread across Chloe's face. "It was so easy."

The grin disappeared. "You weren't supposed to figure this out. You were *supposed* to see the obvious clues and figure out that it was Melissa!"

Scout was getting restless. He clamped down on the edge of Millie's blouse and began to tug. Millie and Scout stood. "Wait here."

The tears began to flow again. "I wish Kyle had lived. Why did he have to die?" Chloe began to wail loudly.

Millie pulled her radio from her belt and lifted it to her lips. "This is Millie Sanders. I'm looking for Dave Patterson.

"Patterson here."

Millie pressed the button. "I need you to meet me outside the entrance to the VIP area. Stat."

She fastened the radio to her belt and stared down at the young woman. "They have to arrest you."

Chloe wiped her eyes with the back of her hand. "I know." She lifted her head defiantly. "I'd rather rot in jail than know Courtney got away with murder."

Courtney get away with murder? Millie shook her head. *Talk about sibling rivalry,* she thought.

Patterson was on deck in no time, accompanied by two somber faced security guards. "Chloe just confessed to killing her sister, Courtney Earhart."

Millie lifted her phone. "I recorded the confession." Millie had heard this was illegal in the U.S. without the other party's consents. Of course, they weren't in the U.S.

The two guards cuffed Chloe and led her away as Scout and Millie looked on. Patterson followed them out.

She patted Scout's head. "I had that one half right."

Millie shuffled into Andy's office. He was sitting at his desk, his head bent over a clipboard.

He dropped the pen and leaned back in his chair when he saw Millie. "Two for two."

Millie let Scout out of his carrier. He promptly wandered around the small office to explore.

She sunk into the chair next to Andy and stuck her fist in her hand. "Not quite. I only had half of it right. Courtney pushed Kyle overboard. When Chloe found out, she was so enraged, she killed her sister."

Andy raised his eyebrows. "Good heavens!"

"I know. Right? On top of that, I almost ran out of time."

"But you didn't," he pointed out. "Speaking of that, it's time to get back to work." He shoved a piece of paper across the table. "I have a new assignment for you."

Millie slipped her reading glasses on and picked up the piece of paper. "What do you mean I have to take a self-defense class?"

Andy leaned back. "If you insist on continuing to live on the edge, you need to learn to protect yourself."

"But..."

"No buts. Meet me in the gym in 45 minutes. Bring your Taser."

The end.

The series continues...Get book 3 at HopeCallaghan.com

Banana Nut Bread

Ingredients
2 eggs
1-1/2 cups sugar
½ cup shortening
1 tsp. vanilla
3 cups flour
2 tsp. baking soda
½ tsp salt
2/3 cup sour milk
3 very ripe bananas
½ cup chopped pecans or walnuts (optional)

*Preheat oven to 325 degrees

1. In large bowl, cream together sugar and shortening. Add eggs and vanilla. Mix well.
2. In separate bowl, mix flour, baking soda and salt
3. Add dry mixture to the creamed mixture of eggs, sugar and shortening, alternating between that and the sour milk and bananas until all are well mixed.
4. Add nuts, if desired.
5. Pour into two lightly greased bread pans.
6. Bake at 325 degrees for one hour or until toothpick, inserted in center of pan, comes out clean.
7. Cool for 15 minutes or drizzle with optional topping (recipe below)

<u>Orange Drizzle (optional)</u>
Bake bread as directed above. Let cool for 10 minutes

Mix: 1 cup powdered sugar, 3 tbsp. fresh orange juice and 1 tsp grated orange rind. Drizzle evenly over warm bread.

About The Author

Hope Callaghan is an author who loves to write Christian books, especially Christian Mystery and Cozy Mystery books. Born and raised in a small town in West Michigan, she now lives in Florida with her husband.

She is the proud mother of one daughter and a stepdaughter and stepson. When she's not doing the thing she loves best - writing books - she enjoys cooking, traveling and reading books.

Hope loves to connect with her readers!

Visit my website for new releases and special offers: http://hopecallaghan.com

Email: hope@hopecallaghan.com

Facebook page:
http://www.facebook.com/hopecallaghanauthor

Other Books by Author, Hope Callaghan:

DECEPTION CHRISTIAN MYSTERY SERIES:

Waves of Deception: Samantha Rite Series Book 1
Winds of Deception: Samantha Rite Series Book 2
Tides of Deception: Samantha Rite Series Book 3

GARDEN GIRLS CHRISTIAN COZY MYSTERIES SERIES:

Who Murdered Mr. Malone?: Book 1
Grandkids Gone Wild: Book 2
Smoky Mountain Mystery: Book 3
Death by Dumplings: Book 4
Eye Spy: Book 5
Magnolia Mansion Mysteries: Book 6
Garden Girls Christian Cozy Mysteries Boxed Set Books 1-4

CRUISE SHIP CHRISTIAN COZY MYSTERIES SERIES:

Starboard Secrets Cruise Ship Cozy Mysteries Book 1

Portside Peril Cruise Ship Cozy Mysteries Book 2

Made in the USA
Las Vegas, NV
22 August 2021

28673534R00184